SCREAMING EAGLES

A High School Football Story

By Mark B. Dengel

Martin Sisters Publishing

Published by

Martin Sisters Publishing, LLC

www. martinsisterspublishing. com

ISBN: 978-1-62553-044-8
Young Adult/Fiction
Printed in the United States of America
Martin Sisters Publishing, LLC

DEDICATION

I would like to dedicate this book to my family. My wife, Bernice, once said the thing she loved about me the most was my ability to tell a story. So I sat down and decided to write one. She has been very patient over the years and has given me the time and space to pursue whatever I desire. I would also like to acknowledge my three children, Alexis, Mitchell, and Sabrina. My kids are very special to me and I want to let them know that I love them very deeply. I want to thank them for making me feel needed and loved in return. To my children, always remember this piece of advice: when your parents make a suggestion for you, the proper response is always, "That is a great idea, I *might* do that."

Chapter 1

Jack Bowden lived in a small house in a seemingly well-to-do neighborhood. Although he could have attended the city's best public school, his mother invested her life savings into putting him and his brother, Sam, into private school. His parents weren't wealthy, but they valued education more than anything.

At seventeen, Jack had grown into a mountain of a man. Standing six foot four and weighing 230 pounds, he commanded attention by virtue of his size. While he was also physically handsome, Jack had many talents. He was an outstanding football player, an accomplished guitarist, and a trusted and loyal friend. Because of his mature appearance and talents, his parents and teachers expected great things from Jack. He always lived up to their standards, but the pressure to perform came with a price. He was often filled with anxiety and spent many hours obsessing on being perfect. His greatest fear was that he might let his family and friends down.

The night before his senior year, Jack was tossing around the football with his little brother in the street in front of their house.

"Go long this time," Sam joked.

"You go long. I've gone long six times in a row and you haven't hit me yet," Jack yelled back still out of breath from his last 30 yard sprint. "How about I go short and see if you can get it within five feet?"

"Down, set, hut one, hut two. Hike the ball, will you Jack?"

Jack passed the football between his legs and then jogged lazily out into the flat. Sam floated a soft spiral, which Jack caught easily with one hand. Jack continued down the street with a hip fake right and a spin to the left. Upon crossing the telephone pole on the left, he raised his hands high in the air and announced, "Touchdown."

Jack proceeded to perform a medley of dance steps. First, the moonwalk, then the robot, and then he finished up with the mashed potato.

While Sam and Jack huddled for the next play, an aging Chevy Malibu pulled into the driveway next door. Jack and Sam both stared as Jenna Witherspoon exited the car. Jack quickly deduced that Jenna was babysitting for the Martins. The Martins had a two year old and he had seen Jenna at the house before.

Jack waved and asked the obvious, "Babysitting again?"

Jenna nodded and responded, "Yeah." Jenna took a few steps toward Jack and continued, "Will I see you at school tomorrow?"

The question, without a doubt, was directed toward Jack. He and Jenna had met the previous May. Jenna was a new student having just moved from Annapolis to Warwick. She had joined

Jack's biology class just before the term ended. Jack was certainly attracted to Jenna. She was as pretty as any girl in school and she always seemed interested in what he had to say. He enjoyed her company so much that he always made a point to speak to her whenever possible.

"Sure," Jack responded, noticing how wonderful Jenna's blonde hair flowed over her shoulders.

Jenna lingered a moment then headed toward the Martins' front door.

"I'm going long and you'd better hit me," Jack said to Sam.

"Down, set, hut one."

Jenna turned around to see Jack running down the street in front of the Martins' house. Sam heaved the ball as far as he could and Jack ran under the ball and casually hauled it in. Jack turned to see if Jenna was watching and she graciously applauded before saying, "Nice catch, but what happened to the touchdown dance?"

Jack's face went red. Apparently, Jenna had seen the last play from her car as she was driving up the street.

Then Sam started in, "Yeah, Jack. What happened to the touchdown dance?"

Jack was now thoroughly embarrassed. After waving to Jenna before she entered the Martins' house, Jack ran after Sam. Sam, sensing danger, began to flee.

"You're dead!" Jack announced as he proceeded to chase Sam around the yard. The pursuit ended with a tackle that swept both boys into the flower garden. Jack, out sizing Sam by nearly 80 pounds, pinned Sam on his back.

"Here's my touchdown dance!" Jack professed as he grabbed handfuls of dirt from the garden, rubbing the damp soil into Sam's hair.

"Stop that right now!" Jack's mother shouted from inside the screen door.

Jack immediately terminated his attack and left Sam for the house. The boys' mother asked for no explanation and neither, Sam nor Jack, offered one. Mrs. Bowden knew that Jack was very fond of Sam and, most of the time, acted as Sam's advocate and protector.

Sam was beginning his freshman year at Sacred Heart and was quite the opposite of Jack. Other than the love of football, they didn't have much in common. Sam, while only fourteen years old, was an intellectual genius. His IQ was tested at 151. Sam often made other kids feel inferior in school because he could articulate on level with his instructors and many times knew answers to questions before they were asked. While Sam was an intellectual giant, he was somewhat physically deficient. He was only five foot six inches and his IQ was more than his weight.

Sam's academic reputation was well founded. Every year, he participated in numerous academic competitions. He won the state spelling bee in the sixth grade, then the city debate championship as a seventh grader, and last year, he won the regional chess tournament.

Sam was very proud of his academic accomplishments, but he loved football. For his entire life, he could remember watching the New England Patriots on Sunday afternoons. Mr. Bowden, Jack, and Sam would gather around the TV and spend the better part of the day cheering the victories and cursing the losses. At halftime, they would go out on the front lawn and throw the ball around. When Sam's internal halftime clock would go off, they would return for the second half kickoff.

Because of the high cost, they never once went to an actual game, but they were faithful fans just the same.

After washing his hands, Jack joined the rest of the family for dinner. The Bowdens were a meat and potatoes family. Rarely did Mrs. Bowden prepare a meal that didn't include mashed potatoes, french fries, or some other heavy starch that accompanied a variety of red meats. Mr. Bowden, Jack, and Sam ordinarily consumed several portions each. Mrs. Bowden always took credit for the size of the male members of the family.

"Another piece of chicken fried steak, Jack?" Mrs. Bowden inquired, offering the serving dish to Jack.

"No, thanks, Mom. I'm already working on my third," Jack answered appreciatively.

"Big day tomorrow, Sam," Mr. Bowden broke in.

"I'm a little nervous, but I expect I'll be better prepared than most of my classmates. All I have to worry about is making it from one class to the next on time; I didn't have an opportunity to look around the building during orientation last June," Sam replied.

"Jack, would you be a dear and look after your little brother?"

"Yes, Mom," Jack answered without hesitation. Jack loved his mother but she didn't even realize what she was doing when she gave him this responsibility. Jack already knew that he was supposed to look out for Sam, but these words made him feel like if something bad happened to Sam, it would be his fault.

"Help me clear the dishes before you start playing," Mrs. Bowden said to everyone.

As a matter of routine, when dinner was finished, Jack retrieved his guitar. He played for his mother while she washed the dishes. At the same time, Mr. Bowden and Sam made their way to the living room for a game of chess.

Jack practiced the guitar more than he practiced football. He loved his guitar and he loved how he could make people smile while he played. He wasn't always this good. Perfection took time, and Jack was determined to make his mom proud of him. He would spend a whole night to master a chord change if that's what it took.

Jack readied himself and began playing the church music his mother loved. After the introductory verse, his mother began to sing the chorus. While Jack also enjoyed singing, he always let his mother lead because he knew how much she enjoyed it. When the song ended, Mrs. Bowden sighed.

"I love that song," proclaimed Mrs. Bowden.

"I know you do. That's why I play it for you," Jack chuckled.

"Play me another."

"What would you like to hear?"

"Surprise me."

After a brief pause to reflect upon his repertoire, Jack plucked slowly and then quickened his pace. His mother quickly recognized the song and began singing with such intensity that laughter came from the living room. Feeling his mother's joy, Jack played louder to match his mother's energy. Mrs. Bowden walked over to Jack as she finished the final hallelujah and gave Jack a big kiss on the cheek. Jack stood, put the guitar on the chair, and hugged his mother.

"Thank you, Jack."

"It's nothing, Mom. I enjoy playing as much as you enjoy singing," Jack said. "I have good news. Father Joseph approached me yesterday after football practice and asked if I would play at Friday's weekly mass for the student body."

"That's wonderful news, Jack!"

"Father gave me a list of songs and I already know most of them. He even said he would give me credit for my music requirement so it will lessen my load."

"Wow. That's great!" Mrs. Bowden exclaimed, "Will I be able to come and watch?"

"Sure," Jack answered with complete confidence.

*

Later that evening, Jack and Sam went to bed with great anticipation for the next day.

"What's high school like?" Sam asked Jack from the top bunk.

"Shut up and quit bugging me," Jack mumbled.

"But I need to know. I need to fit in," Sam pleaded.

Jack thought for a long while, reflecting on his own freshman year recalling how small he seemed compared to the upperclassmen, the teachers, and even the building itself.

"The best advice I can give you is to keep your mouth shut. Don't show off about how smart you are. Everyone will know in time. Don't show people up. You aren't going to high school to learn. If that was the idea, then you could just go to the library and read. High school is about relating to other people. High school is about making a few good friends and being able to hang out and share good times."

Jack laid there contemplating his own words then kicked the top bunk from underneath. "Now, will you shut up and go to sleep?"

*

Sam followed Jack from the car to the entrance of the high school. Jack turned to Sam as he opened the front door and said, "Brace yourself Sam . . . for the best time of your life."

Sam looked at Jack in disbelief.

High School had been a blessing for Jack. Jack was a High School All-American Football Player his junior year. He had grown 8 inches in the past two years and was presently dating Wendy Thompson, the most beautiful and desired girl at Sacred Heart High School. Jack was popular with both the faculty and the student body. Jack couldn't be more fortunate.

Sam understood that this was the best time of Jack's life and that his own high school days were just beginning.

The hallway was crowded with hundreds of students. Some were digging in their lockers. Others were gathered in small groups talking all at the same time. Some were just passing, looking for stretch of space to occupy.

A bell rang and Jack looked at an overhead clock and then at his watch. He looked up and saw Wendy walking down the hall toward him, flanked on both sides by her best friends, Sue Rich and Kelly Singer. Wendy flipped her hair from side to side as she walked.

Wendy and her friends were in their glory, parading about the school. Their new clothes complemented their glistening hair. Their broad smiles showed off their perfectly straight white teeth. Each wore matching green and blue plaid jumper uniforms with a little Sacred Heart emblem on the left breast pocket. As they passed down the corridor they waved, smiled, and greeted others like royalty greeting subjects.

As they approached Jack, Wendy broke into a little gallop and outstretched her arms for a romantic embrace that Jack reciprocated. Wendy had to leave her feet in order for Jack to

12

pull her in. Jack spun Wendy in a tight circle, kissing her lightly on the cheek.

"Hi, Jack. I missed you," Wendy announced to Jack, making sure her friends heard their conversation.

"I missed you, too, Wendy. It's been, what . . . a whole week since you went to New York?" Jack mused.

Wendy ignored Jack's sarcasm. "What class do you have now?" Wendy inquired, taking Jack's schedule to compare to her own. "Oh look, we both have English with Ms. Thomas. We'll have a great time in her class."

"Hey, Sue, Kelly, do you guys know my little brother, Sam?" Jack asked while Wendy continued to analyze their schedules.

Sue and Kelly both nodded their heads passively. They had met Sam last spring when they had come over to the Bowden's house to see Jack.

"Sam, this is Kelly and Sue," Jack said, pointing them out as if it were important for Sam to remember.

Sam remained silent as Wendy started up again. "Oh, shoot. Our first classes are on opposite ends of the building. This is a real bummer."

Jack smiled and agreed, "Bummer."

Wendy frowned. "You don't seem upset?"

"Yeah, it breaks me up that I won't be able to carry your books up two flights of stairs. That's a tough break, Wendy. Maybe you should go to the principal's office and have my schedule changed," Jack joked as a second bell rang. "I'll see you at lunch, Wendy," Jack said, letting go of her and backing away. "By the way, you look great."

Wendy smiled. She knew she was beautiful but she still needed to be told so. And Jack wasn't stretching the truth. She was as pretty as ever. Her skin was unblemished and tanned;

her hair was striking, shining even in the dim light of the hallway. Her uniform was pressed neatly and fit snugly against her athletic body. As Wendy twirled and walked away, she shouted so everyone could hear, "I love you, Jack!"

Jack laughed right out loud. He put his hand on Sam's shoulder and said, "Let me show you to your first class."

Having Jack by his side as they walked through the hallways made Sam feel very important. His brother was a celebrity. Every person that passed them said something to Jack. The students that didn't know Sam were introduced and Sam had somewhat of an instant status within the school.

*

Sam chose a seat in the rear of Advanced Algebra. He knew right away that this class would be filled mostly with juniors and seniors. The boys that sat around him all seemed to be twice his size, and the girls looked more like women than schoolgirls.

While Sam preferred to remain anonymous, he could easily see he was going to stick out like a sore thumb. His jacket was only a 36 and it hung on him like a coat hanger while his tie was so long that it hung down beneath his fly. When he put his hand to his face to provide greater obscurity, he felt his acne which created an even wider physical disparity between him and the other students.

The instructor wrote his name on the board before taking role. Mr. Stamps, his newly identified teacher, began to call names one by one. After each name was called, a student would say 'here,' and like a chain reaction, all heads would immediately turn to the respondent.

"Sam Bowden," Mr. Stamps called.

"Here," Sam answered.

All eyes were now cast upon him. Some girls smiled and others giggled. The boys' expressions were stone cold.

One boy, however, blurted out, "You must be lost. The elementary school is across the street."

The class erupted with laughter.

Sam's ears turned bright red and his eyes welled up.

Mr. Stamps paused and continued the role.

"Chuck Cruise," Mr. Stamps called.

"Present," said the boy who had made the joke about Sam.

Sam sat up and began to make observations about this boy. Chuck Cruise was a boy who had all the confidence in the world. He was tall and well groomed. His face had sharp lines and his expressions varied widely as he communicated in silence with several other boys who sat around him.

Instruction began shortly thereafter. Mr. Stamps began with a review of binominals. He bore down on the board with his white chalk as he produced problem after problem. The students around Sam labored trying to keep up.

Sam, in contrast, was a master mathematician. He was only in this class because the school offered only a limited variety of advanced math courses. After seeing the pattern of problems Mr. Stamps introduced, Sam didn't feel the need to write down every problem. He decided it would be sufficient to only write down the moderately difficult sets.

Mr. Stamps looked up and saw Sam sitting idle while the other students were hard at work, copying a new equation from the board.

"Mr. Bowden, what seems to be the matter?" Mr. Stamps questioned.

"I'm sorry?" Sam replied, taken by surprise.

"I see you have already lost interest in the class 15 minutes into the term," Mr. Stamps said with thick disdain.

"No, sir. I'm interested. I just didn't know we were supposed to write everything down," Sam stuttered.

"I suggest you write it down unless you already know it," Mr. Stamps sneered.

While everyone turned back to their own work, Sam suffered. He was experiencing intense internal conflict during his first class, on his first day, in this new school. He thought about what Jack had said the night before about keeping his mouth shut and fitting in. He knew he didn't fit in. He wasn't normal and he wasn't going to be treated in this disrespectful manner by both the teacher and the other students. Sam made his mind up right there to take on the world. He laid his pencil down and folded his arms.

Mr. Stamps turned back toward the class and again saw Sam sitting upright as everyone else was slumped over their notebooks.

"So, Mr. Bowden, from your disposition, I can assume you already know this material," Mr. Stamps remarked. "Can you provide us with the solution to this problem?"

"Yes sir, I can." Sam paused for dramatic affect and said, "X = -4."

Mr. Stamps looked at Sam with disgust and muttered, "Correct."

The class gasped and Sam felt a rush of satisfaction.

Cruise turned his head and said directly to Sam, "Way to go, geek."

After Cruise turned back around to face the instructor, a girl sitting directly across the aisle smiled at Sam and whispered, "He's such an asshole."

Sam decided he should appease Mr. Stamps and at least pretend to take vigorous notes. In the midst of class, he found Mr. Stamps looking in his direction. Mr. Stamps cracked a smile that only Sam could see. Sam grinned and quickly returned to his notes.

Chapter 2

The cafeteria was alive with activity. Students were bustling about. As some students waited in line for their lunch, others were cleaning up and returning to class. The constant turnover of students seemed confusing on the surface, but the design always provided enough seating and time for students to eat a sociable lunch.

Because Sam's friends from the 8th grade all attended public school, he felt alone at Sacred Heart among the other 600 students. After filling his tray, Sam walked toward a table filled with students that appeared by their physical size to be freshmen. Sam pulled up a chair at the end of the table and began to eat in silence. Before he even took his third bite, the entire table of students simultaneously stood, lifted their lunch trays, and walked to the exit.

The noise associated with the mass exit drew the attention of the surrounding tables. Sam felt more alone than ever. The fact that every table except his was almost completely full made him even more self-conscious. At this point, he felt like everyone was watching him and he became filled with anxiety.

As more and more students entered the lunch line, Sam believed it was only a matter of time before one of them would sit at his table. One by one, the students passed him by for a different table. Each minute that passed seemed like an eternity. Sam began to perspire from the brow and his face went pale. He lowered his head to shield his shame.

"Excuse me, is this seat taken?"

Sam looked up and before him was Jenna Witherspoon.

"No, no. Please sit down," Sam said with great relief.

Sam's emotions shifted instantaneously. Not only had he been rescued from this horrible social embarrassment, but he had been saved by Jenna Witherspoon.

"Do you mind if a few of my friends sit here as well?" she asked as she placed her tray on the table.

Before Sam had a chance to respond, five more stunning young ladies surrounded him. Sam glanced at each one as they took their seats.

Jenna politely introduced Sam to her friends. "This is Sam Bowden, Jack Bowden's little brother. Sam, this is Victoria, Hannah, Moriah, Jillian, and Sarah."

Sam looked in the direction of each girl as Jenna introduced them.

When Sarah saw Sam, she exclaimed, "You're that guy from my Algebra class! Oh, my God! That was so great how you showed up Mr. Stamps. That's never happened around here before."

"That was you!" Jenna cut in, having been previously informed of the event. "Oh my God! I can't wait to tell Jack."

Sarah suddenly remarked, "How about Chuck Cruise? What an idiot! I can't believe he said those things to you. He's got everything in the whole world. Why would anyone act like that?"

"Maybe he was abused when he was younger?" Sam hypothesized.

"I used to live on the same street as him when we were in elementary school," Sarah began. "He had everything. But it seemed like the only thing he enjoyed was watching other people's pain. One time he dug a hole about three feet deep and covered it with sticks, newspaper and dirt. After he camouflaged it like a tiger trap, he lured my brother's friend over it by offering him a piece of candy. The kid didn't see the false top and he fell in. He hurt himself really bad. Chuck thought it was the funniest thing ever. The kid limped home crying and Chuck was still laughing."

"That is the cruelest thing I've ever heard," Moriah added.

"When he was older, he would put seeds on the rock wall behind his house. When squirrels would come to eat the seeds, he would shoot them with his bb gun for fun," Sarah stated as a matter of fact.

"I hate that guy," Hannah declared. "I used to date him last year. He was so rude. The day I broke up with him was the best day of my life."

Jenna smiled at Sam and said, "I guess you're not the only one who doesn't have any affection for Chuck Cruise."

Sam shrugged, "Guess not."

Sam proceeded to sit back and listen to the girls' converse about classes, clothes, and boys.

*

"Hi Jack," Wendy sang right before she threw her arms around Jack and kissed him on the cheek. "Meet me on the west side steps at 3:00. I need a ride home tonight."

"Sorry, Wendy. I've got football practice right after school," Jack said, shaking his head.

"You can be late," Wendy smirked.

"Not that late." Jack said, still shaking his head no.

"Give me your keys... you can walk home after practice. I'll give you back your car tomorrow," Wendy said, assuming Jack wouldn't refuse.

"Okay, Wendy. Be nice to her. She's parked in the south lot," Jack responded, handing over the keys to his red Firebird.

"What a witch!" Victoria whispered to Jenna after eavesdropping on Wendy and Jack's exchange.

"I know...right," Jenna said, watching Wendy walk away from Jack.

Jack turned and approached Jenna and Victoria. Victoria waited until Jack was right upon them before she threw her arms around Jenna in the same way Wendy did with Jack. "Hi Jack," Victoria mimicked. "Give me your car and...you can walk home."

Jenna and Victoria doubled over laughing and fell into the lockers making a loud crash.

Jenna was relieved to see Jack was amused.

"I hope you two are having a good time," Jack said, giving Victoria a light punch in the arm. "Are you guys in chemistry lab right now?" Jack asked, hoping they were.

"Yeah, you?" Jenna responded.

"Yes I am." Jack answered with enthusiasm. "We should be lab partners."

"No, I don't think so," Victoria said, trying to get under Jenna's skin.

Jenna hip checked Victoria in a playful manner. "She's just playing with you. We'd be honored to be lab partners with you. Wouldn't we, Vic?"

"Yeah, whatever," Victoria said, spinning toward the class.

*

The locker room smelled of sweat and mildew. The football players were casually changing into their practice gear when Jack strolled through. Met with nods of acknowledgement from his teammates, Jack made his way to the coach's office.

Jack knocked on the door.

"Enter," a voice commanded from the other side.

Jack opened the door to find his head football coach putting his whistle around his neck.

Coach Dawson was an imposing man. While his playing days were far behind him, he still loved the game. He was an enormous man that tested his players both physically and mentally. He worked them to the breaking point. They practiced in the summer heat with full pads for two and a half hours twice a day with full contact. The more they begged for relief, the more he worked them. Because his reputation was well known after ten seasons at Sacred Heart, only the heartiest souls came out for the team.

"Coach, can I have a minute?" Jack asked rather formally.

"Sure, anything for my MVP," Coach Dawson said, trying to lighten the mood.

Jack was indeed last year's most valuable player. He started every game at middle linebacker and was the strong hold of the best defense in the state. Leading the Screaming Eagles to a 9-3 record the previous season, Jack personally led the defense in almost every statistical category. He recorded the most tackles, sacks, forced fumbles and fumble recoveries. In addition to being a fierce hitter, he was the fastest and strongest player on the team. Jack was clearly the best player and Coach Dawson was well aware that their state championship hopes depended on a repeat performance by his star linebacker.

"I want to ask you a favor," Jack said, waiting for a signal to continue.

"What? What is it? Get it out boy. I don't have all day."

"I want to know if I can get my little brother on the team," Jack asked, half expecting his request to be rejected.

"How come he didn't try out with everyone else two weeks ago when training camp started?"

"He's kind of small and didn't think he would make the team. He's a freshman. Since you didn't have to cut anyone, I thought you might consider it."

"It just wouldn't be fair, Jack. Doesn't he realize how long and hard you boys have been working up to this point?"

"It's not really his idea Coach. It's mine. He doesn't know I'm asking," Jack shrugged. "I just wanted to get my kid brother involved in school. So he would be a part of something good."

"Damn it, Jack!" Coach Dawson scolded. "What position does he play?"

"Quarterback."

"Quarterback...Holy hell! How's he going to learn the plays with only a week before the first game?"

"He's real smart, Coach. I know he can do it," Jack stated, knowing his brother's abilities.

"Well, it doesn't matter. He won't play the first three games anyway. He'll be third string after that because there is no fourth string," Dawson said, chuckling at his own joke.

Coach Dawson turned away from Jack to gather his clipboard and pencil, then he set the final condition, "By the way, he'll have to go through the meat grinder. You think he's up for that?"

The meat grinder was a drill conducted in practice when one player would line up seven yards away from a defensive opponent and try to get by them with the ball. The catch was that the player carrying the ball would have to line up opposite every member of the team one after the other. Usually, the ball carrier would become so exhausted after the first few defenders; he would end up taking a beating by the end of the drill. On top of all that, the biggest, toughest, and meanest players on the team took places at the end of the line. The drill was generally reserved for players who committed critical errors such as penalties, fumbles, dropped passes or missed blocks.

This time the meat grinder was being administered for acceptance. Sam couldn't join the team two weeks late without some type of penalty. But Jack knew the mental toughness of his younger brother. Sam could take all Jack had and come back for more. Sure, Jack always got the better of him when they fought, but it didn't discourage Sam from challenging him again and again.

"No problem Coach. If there's anything I can do for you, let me know," Jack replied, reaching for the door to let himself out.

"Say Jack, there is one small thing…can you win me a state title this year?"

Jack smiled. Shaking his head side to side, Jack thought about Coach Dawson's last words. The coach said it as a joke, but Jack knew he was serious. If their team was going to be successful, it would be up to Jack to make it happen. He knew the coach, the players and the student body were expecting a championship season and it was up to him to deliver one.

*

Alone at his locker and gathering his things, Sam shook his head thinking about his homework. He'd had as much before, but never on the first day of school. As much as he hated spending his time reading textbooks, he hated lugging them home even more.

"Sam!" Jack yelled as he came jogging down the hall wearing his football gear.

"What?" Sam retorted, still miffed about the workload.

"Whatcha doing?" Jack asked, knowing it was nothing important.

"What do you want now?" Sam asked in a suspecting tone.

"Want to come out for the football team?" Jack smiled.

"No," Sam replied.

"Come on. It'll be fun...make some friends...get to know people."

"It's too late. Coach wouldn't let me even if I wanted to."

"Not a problem. I already asked. He said it was okay. He said you'd have to sit out the first three games, but after that, you'd be all set. What do you say?"

Sam thought about it. He wanted to say yes. It wouldn't be that big of a stretch. He'd played Pop Warner the past two years. He knew the rules and strategies better than anyone. Sam also thought about why he hadn't tried out for the team. It wasn't because he was too small as he had told his family, but because he didn't excel at football at the same level as he did with his other activities. After being hailed the most intelligent kid at his middle school, his gridiron prowess was minimal compared to his academic achievements. In spite of his love for the game, he knew he would never be a great football player. So, he simply gave it up.

Sam raised his head and said, "Okay, but you gotta tell Mom it was your idea."

"Not a problem." Jack responded, thinking it was kind of her idea that he look after Sam.

*

By the time Sam made his way to the locker room and found the equipment manager, practice was already half over. Sam jogged casually from the locker room to the practice field with his helmet on, trying not to be noticed.

Sam saw Coach Dawson across the field and ran directly to him. As Sam increased his pace toward Coach Dawson, he could vaguely hear comments directed at him.

"Fresh meat," one player said.

"He's mine. I'll have him for breakfast," said another.

Sam began to sweat when he reached Coach Dawson. He stood by patiently as Coach Dawson directed the offense through its passing game. Sam observed the offense and most notably, the quarterback. The first pass play was a quick hitting crossing route over the middle. The next play was a sideline route and then a deep post. The quarterback hit all three receivers in stride. He had nimble feet and a quick release. Sam was thoroughly impressed.

Coach Dawson clapped his hands after the third reception along with the rest of the offense. "Way to go Cruise...looking good... looking good."

Sam's jaw dropped. Chuck Cruise was the starting quarterback. The same Chuck Cruise that had insulted him earlier in the day. Sam wanted to be somewhere else...anywhere else.

Then Coach Dawson turned to Sam and said, "So, you're Jack Bowden's kid brother. Good to see you. Glad to have you on the team."

When Coach Dawson blew his whistle, the entire team came running and quickly made a line on the 30 yard line. Sam was a little confused until an assistant coach laid out four orange cones, tossed Sam the ball and said, "You start here." Sam then recognized the drill and became a bit frightened.

While Sam was adjusting his gear, Jack appeared from the mass of football laden boys. Jack put his arm around Sam and said, "It's a kind of compensation...it's the only way you could be on the team. Sorry I didn't mention it earlier. A bit of advice...stay low... and don't fumble."

Just before the drill began, Coach Dawson yelled to his team. "Strap it on boys. Don't hold back!"

The team's loud affirmation was muffled only by their engaged mouthpieces.

At the front of the line stood Jack. Jack had to prove that his loyalty to the team would not be undermined by anything, even his own brother. He was the leader of the team and in order to keep their trust and respect, he had to set the standard of football integrity. Sam understood this positioning and also understood that if he could take Jack's best shot, he could handle any hit.

The whistle blew and both boys accelerated off the line. Sam felt his body compress when Jack laid his shoulder into his chest. The air raced from Sam's lungs. The thunderous blow took Sam's feet from under him and propelled him backward. Jack wrapped his arms around Sam's torso and stuck him all the way into the ground. When they hit the turf, the impact was excruciating.

The coaches and players looked on in shock. They had never witnessed such a vicious, merciless hit in all their lives. Some turned away while others moaned in sympathy. The whole team went quiet. They just stared at Sam like he was unrecognizable road kill.

Sam lay motionless as Jack lifted himself from his brother. Sam opened his eyes and saw Jack's outstretched hand. While Jack helped Sam to his feet, Sam moaned and uttered, "It'll be fun…you'll make some friends…get to know people. Thanks. Thanks a lot."

The worst was over and Sam knew it would only get easier from this point. Sam stumbled back to his predetermined position and readied himself. When the next player got into position, Sam lurched forward at the coach's whistle and smashed square into his opponent's chest. Both players tumbled to the dirt. Player after player hit him. At first, the meat grinder seemed an impossible undertaking but as the line of defenders dwindled, Sam actually gained confidence. Instead of tiring, he gained momentum. He began to break tackles and leave defenders lying in his wake. Sam began to hear clapping following each confrontation.

Three Screaming Eagles remained. Chuck Cruise and his buddies were slapping each other on their shoulder pads attempting to psych themselves into monster hits on Sam. Each of the three seniors was about the size of Jack and clearly intended to show Sam no mercy.

The first of the trio was Billy Hamilton. He was a large brute that was as much fat as he was muscle. Hamilton, who played offensive tackle, tipped the scale at 260. Hamilton was known for his dirty play. Often times, he would bite other players at the bottom of a pile or step on an ankle of a player that was still on the ground. He was guilty of holding on almost every play and always seemed to get away with it. His own team hated him because his antics occurred in practice as frequently as they did in games.

"I'm going to make you cry like a girl," Hamilton snorted out of the oversized facemask that shielded his fat head.

The two boys lined up and moved forward simultaneously. Sam went low and planted his helmet into Hamilton's groin. Hamilton grunted like a pig, and then fell silent. He rolled off Sam's back and into the fetal position. He groaned in agony.

The rest of the team broke into a chorus of laughter. The defensive players, the ones that despised Hamilton the most, were in hysterics. They began falling down and rolling on the ground laughing at the disabled bully.

Coach Dawson became irritated. He knew the type of player Hamilton was, but he didn't want the team to lose its unity. While he was aware that friction existed between the offense and defense, he also knew that if players were allowed to publicly embarrass members of the other side, the divide would become greater.

"That'll be enough gentlemen. Watson, Smith and Johnson get up and give me fifty," Coach Dawson barked. "Coach Williams, would you please take Hamilton to the locker room?"

Next up was Chuck's best friend Matt Singleton. Singleton was the starting tailback on last year's team. Unlike Hamilton, Singleton was all muscle and was widely known for his sportsmanship. It was ironic that Singleton was such good friends with Cruise and Hamilton because his character was completely the opposite. Everyone assumed that Singleton and Cruise were such good friends because they grew up in the same neighborhood.

Singleton charged off the line at the whistle. Singleton leveled Sam as everyone had expected. The impact left Sam grimacing. Sam rolled over and slowly staggered back to his line.

Up stepped Chuck Cruise to a mixed response. The offense cheered and the defense booed. Chuck had a tight circle of friends and they all played offense. The defense, however, still blamed Chuck for blowing their chance for a state title last year. They felt he cost them their opportunity by fumbling late in fourth quarter in the semifinals. The fumble happened with two minutes left on their own eight yard line. At the time, Sacred Heart was up by two points. The Toll Gate Titans kicked a field goal and went on to win the championship.

Chuck walked up to Sam and said, "You're nothing but a punk. We don't even want you on this team and you will certainly never play quarterback as long as I'm here."

Sam didn't say anything. He just waited for Cruise to go back to his spot.

Once Cruise got set, Sam waited for the whistle but Cruise didn't. He left his mark clearly before the whistle blew and was on top of Sam before he moved two steps. Sam felt his shoulder pop and winced in pain as he went down.

When Sam hit the ground, Jack knew something was wrong and sprinted over to him. He lifted Cruise off his brother.

"You alright Sam?" Jack asked with great concern.

"No...I think my shoulder is dislocated," Sam replied.

"He'll be alright. He's just a wuss," Cruise taunted.

Jack stood up and thrust both hands into Cruise's chest, sending him to the ground. Before Cruise could get to his feet, the coaches intervened. Two players and Coach Dawson had to restrain Jack from attacking Cruise a second time.

"You're a freakin' idiot," Jack cursed, shaking off those holding him back.

"It's just football. You've got to be able to take a hit." Cruise answered back, playing the part of a victim.

"Shut up!" Coach Dawson yelled at both players. "That's enough for today. Hit the showers."

The team jogged off the field together, but they were clearly divided now more than ever.

Chapter 3

The five boys sat on the steps of the school long after everyone else had gone home. Practice had ended 45 minutes ago and Sam, Jack and Jack's three friends, Tim Watson, Mark Johnson, and Ken Smith were all that remained.

"When are you going to get your car back?" Sam asked Jack, half annoyed.

"Wendy said she would need it just one more day," Jack answered.

"What time did you say she was going to pick us up?" Sam continued.

"She said six o'clock."

Looking at his watch, Sam noted the time, "She's a half-hour late. Should we wait or start walking?"

"Let's wait another 15 minutes."

Sam adjusted the sling around his left arm. It had been three days since Chuck had dislocated his shoulder and it still didn't feel much better.

Noticing Sam's discomfort, Mark inquired about his condition, "How's the shoulder?"

"Hurts when I move it. I'll be able to take the sling off in two weeks," Sam said, appreciating the attention.

"That's too bad. Cruise is such a dork. I'd hate to play offense. I don't know how you can take it," Mark confessed. "I really lucked out when Coach asked me to play safety last year. I almost turned him down."

"I know what you mean," Ken agreed. "I played both ways last year on the line. When we were in the huddle, everyone argued and Chuck was always crying about something."

Sam had heard these gripes before at home, but now he was living it. "How come you guys don't go after him during our scrimmages?"

"What are you saying? Do you think they tell us the plays before they run them?" Ken asked, becoming defensive.

"Are you saying you can't tell what play is coming?" Sam asked in surprise.

"Do you think we're mind readers?" Mark smirked, taking Ken's side.

"Have you guys ever actually read our playbook?" Sam went on, opening his own playbook.

"No. Why would we? We play defense," Ken declared, stating the obvious.

"Look at this," Sam said, showing Mark an outline the team's offensive plays. "We only have ten formations, three with motion. Of those, we throw out of four. If you recognize the formation and situation, you can predict pass or run ninety percent of the time."

"Holy crap! Give me that playbook," Ken demanded, ripping it from Sam's hands. "If Cruise doesn't get hurt in tomorrow's game, he will for sure on Monday."

"I hope that playbook is easier to read than my algebra book," Tim said as he flipped through his book looking for his assignment. "Hey Sam, can you give me a hand with this algebra?"

"Sure," Sam replied, leaning over Tim's notebook.

"I'm having a real hard time. I never get the right answer and the examples in the book are useless."

Sam examined Tim's work and saw instantly where his errors occurred. "You have to square both sides of the equation before you can divide. All the problems on this page use the same principles. If you can remember to perform the same function on both sides of the equation, you really can't go wrong."

"Thanks, Sam. You're a real geek!" Tim exclaimed.

Sam looked confused.

"In a good way," Tim clarified.

Jack smiled to himself watching his little brother tutor his friends. Sam was always the smartest kid in the class, but now he was using his brain. He was becoming important to the guys and Jack knew that would pay big dividends for Sam in the future.

Jack, on the other hand, wasn't the best student in high school. While it was certainly true that he always put forth a strong effort when he studied, he was a B student at best. He had a deal with his teachers. Jack would always attend class, complete all assignments, pay attention and regardless of his test scores, he would get a B.

The deal was that all of the students in the class remained calm during instruction or Jack would act as the enforcer of order. When the boys in the class would get loud, Jack would ask them to "be cool" and they did. He didn't have a reputation of being a violent person, but the other kids did not want a confrontation with the alpha male.

"Hey, we should get together and make a study group," Mark suggested.

"Yeah, that would be great," Ken agreed. "I could bring the food, Mark can bring the drinks and Tim could bring the girls. We can't really study without girls…you know…motivation."

Jack laid on the grass. "This is great. My friends like my little brother more than me. I seriously have to get some new friends."

"We don't like him more. We just need him more," Tim corrected as he got to his feet. "But we'll always love you, Jack."

With that, Tim threw himself on top of Jack. Seeing this, Ken and Mark joined in and jumped on the pile.

Jack wrestled his way free from the three boys and leapt to his feet.

"Do that again and I'll kill all of you," Jack threatened. "Come on, Sam. Let's start walking."

*

The soda can stood upright and Jack claimed victory. "That's seven to two, I win."

"I don't get it," Sam wondered aloud. "How can you win every time? If there were some physics involved, I'd know it. How can you be so lucky?"

"It's not luck. I practice kicking cans all the time," Jack joked.

Eyeballing the dented soda can, Sam took a three step gallop and kicked it toward a drain on the side of the street. The can bounced twice before landing in the gutter.

Grinning with some degree of satisfaction, Sam changed the subject. "How do you think we'll do tomorrow against East Greenwich?"

"If the offense can hang onto the ball, we should win easily," Jack predicted. "Our first real test is going to be against Pilgrim next Friday. They're always tough and they're returning 8 of 11 starters on offense. Remember that stuff you were talking about...how you can tell what play our offense is going to run? If we had film of Pilgrim, could you tell with them? You know... what play is coming before they run it?"

"It depends on how complicated their offense is," Sam shrugged. "Can you get someone to film their game this weekend?"

"I think so. I'll ask the coach," Jack replied as his Firebird came tearing around the corner.

Both Jack and Sam moved quickly up onto the grass to avoid being run down. The car skidded to a stop beside them. The window retracted and music blasted from the car. Wendy and Sue danced in their seats to Jack's Meatloaf CD.

"Praying for the end of time, so I can end my time with you!" they both sang while they pretended to slap each other in the face. Their musical folly was clearly a production for the two boys.

When the song ended, Wendy turned to Jack and asked in her cute but fake southern drawl, "You boys see any football players 'round these parts?"

Jack smiled and forgot all about Wendy's tardiness when she opened the door and stepped out of the car. She made up for her lack of punctuality by wearing skin tight jeans that rode up her rear and a shirt that exposed her tight abs. On top of that, she provided Jack with a romantic embrace for his unending generosity. When she gave Jack a long deep wet kiss, all was forgiven.

"Come on already!" Sue shouted from within the car.

"Patience darling, we'll be right with you," Wendy responded, giving Jack another passionate kiss.

The couple separated and Jack opened the passenger door for Wendy. Sue had already vacated the front seat for the back when Wendy asked, "You don't mind if I drive, do you Jack?"

Shaking his head, Jack grinned and got in the passenger seat. With Sam already in the car, Wendy ran around the front and slid into the driver's seat. She gunned the engine and popped the clutch. The tires spun wildly and the back fishtailed from side to side as the four teenagers screamed with both fear and excitement. Smoke filled the air and rubber burned on the pavement. Wendy raced down the street like she had done it a thousand times before.

"What took you guys so long?" Sam questioned in a demanding tone.

"Sue needed a haircut and the salon was packed," Wendy replied with no remorse.

"You left us hanging…for a haircut," Sam remarked in total disgust.

Wendy locked up the brakes and skidded to an abrupt halt, creating an equal amount of noise and smoke as when she peeled out.

She turned to Jack's younger brother in the back seat. "You just shut the hell up! If you don't like it, just get the hell out and walk, you ungrateful little turd."

Sam looked at Jack for some backup but got none. Sam looked back at Wendy and cursed her under his breath.

Wendy laid on the gas again and they were off.

*

"Please pass the salad," Wendy asked Sam in her sweetest voice.

Sam passed the salad thinking how unbelievable it was that Wendy could change personalities so quickly. It had been only 30 minutes since she went ballistic on him in the car and now she was being so civil.

"Are you going to the football game tomorrow, Wendy?" Mr. Bowden asked, assuming she would.

"Oh, yes. I'm the captain of the cheerleading squad this year. I'll be right down in front, cheering our team to victory."

"Have you girls been working on any new routines for this season?" Mrs. Bowden asked, trying to make Wendy feel as welcome as possible.

"Definitely. We're doing a really cool dance routine at halftime. I just wish Jack would be able to see it. It's a shame the football team has to go to the locker room during our performance."

"Yeah, it's a shame," Sam added sarcastically through a mouthful of potatoes.

"Jack, how's the defense shaping up?" Jack's father continued.

"We'll be okay," Jack said, trying to be modest. "I think we'll win."

"Are you suiting up for the game?" Mr. Bowden asked Sam, looking at his bandaged arm.

"Yeah. I'm number 10. I'll wave to you from the sidelines," Sam answered between bites of his chicken leg.

"Wendy, would you like some chicken?" Mrs. Bowden offered as she attempted to put a thigh on Wendy's plate.

"Oh, no thank you. I'm trying watch what I eat," Wendy replied, putting a frown on Mrs. Bowden's face.

Wendy could feel the tension during the silence that followed. She looked at her watch and remarked, "Oh my goodness, I've got a hair appointment at 8 o'clock. I've really got to run."

When she excused herself from the table, Jack followed her out.

"I'll give your car back to you tomorrow," Wendy said before she hopped in the car and sped away.

When Jack reentered the house, his mother was enraged.

"What was that?" his mother demanded in front of the whole family.

"What?" Jack played dumb.

"I invite Wendy over for dinner. You three waltz in here an hour late and then she doesn't even try the chicken. Can you explain that?" Mrs. Bowden asked, throwing her arms about as she talked.

"I can't. I'm sorry, Mom. She doesn't know you all that well and maybe she's a little shy," Jack said in Wendy's defense. "She's a terrific person. If you'd just give her another chance, I'm sure you'll end up liking her as much as I do. I'm sorry things went so bad."

Sam opened his mouth to offer an opposing opinion of Wendy, but opted to keep it to himself. He didn't believe for a moment that his mom was buying Jack's load of crap, so he didn't need to participate in the discussion.

Jack understood his mom's frustration, but he couldn't take sides between his mom and his girlfriend. He decided it would be best to just to keep them away from each other. The conflict was giving him anxiety so he attempted to distract his mother with her favorite activity.

"Can I play a song for you?" Jack asked upon retrieving his guitar.

"Don't you need to practice for Mass tomorrow?" his mother reminded him.

Jack leaned over, kissed his mother and said, "Oh yeah, thanks."

*

Clutching his well-worn acoustic guitar, Jack began to review the pieces of music he was to play at this morning's Mass. Standing at the podium overlooking the chapel was a new perspective for him. Empty now, students would begin filling the church within the hour. Jack went right to work rehearsing. As he masterfully changed chords, he strummed his guitar with smooth even strokes. He began to sing at a low level and then louder to match the volume at which he played. Soon, he was oblivious to his surroundings and concentrated exclusively on the music.

All at once, his voice seemed distorted as the words he sang echoed back six-fold. He looked up from his music and saw his friends dancing up the center aisle of the church singing along with him. Jack lost his place momentarily and then joined his friend's exaggerated enthusiasm. His voice boomed off the marble columns as he played his guitar with the energy of a rock concert. "Kum bay ya, my lord, Kum bay ya," they all sang together at the top of their lungs.

When the song was over, Jack exchanged high fives with the guys. "What are you guys doing here so early?"

"We came to hear you play," Mark said, nodding in Jenna's direction. "Jenna has never seen you play. It was her idea."

Jack smiled at Jenna and Jenna blushed in return.

"You play great," Jenna remarked, wishing she had something better to say.

"You don't mind if we sit in the front row?" Tim asked after he had already planted himself.

"No, go ahead. It's nice to see friendly faces. I hope you don't mind if I keep playing until Mass starts," Jack returned, positioning his guitar on his hip.

"Can you play a little AC/DC?" Tim asked without religious concern.

"Here?" Jack objected.

"Go ahead. No one is even here. It'll sound great." Tim reassured him.

Jenna smiled and gave him the thumbs up.

Jack shrugged and started to play the introduction to 'Highway to Hell'.

The kids began to do a head banging motion and raised the rock and roll fingers to the music. When Jack came to the chorus, he noticed other people coming through the front door. Jack switched back to the scripted music instantaneously. When his friends booed him, he just smiled and continued to play as the student body trickled into the chapel for the 10 a.m. service.

Jenna, Victoria, and Hannah sat with Mark, Tim and Ken in the first pew. They admired Jack's talents openly. The girls swayed from side to side in sync hoping to draw his attention. Jack noticed the girls staring at him. He really liked Jenna and they had become good friends in the three short days he was her chemistry partner. He suspected she wanted to date him, but both of them respected his existing relationship with Wendy.

Often Jack scanned the congregation expecting to locate Wendy. He hoped she would be present to hear him play. Then right before the processional, he saw more familiar faces. His mother and Sam walked up the side and moved into the first pew along with his friends. Jack's mother sat right next to Jenna.

Jenna had seen Mrs. Bowden before and easily recognized her. Jenna slid toward the center of the pew to allow Mrs. Bowden more room. She greeted Mrs. Bowden with a whisper. When Mrs. Bowden knelt to pray, Jenna knelt alongside her wanting to make a good impression. Sensing Jenna's motive, Hannah and Victoria also knelt.

Mrs. Bowden could see the three girls kneeling together through the corner of her eye. Each girl wore her hair perfectly straight with a black headband. With the girls also wearing matching plaid uniforms, they could have nearly passed for triplets. All three girls knelt in exactly the same position; with their backs perfectly straight, their hands clasped together, their heads up and their eyes closed. None made a sound. Their demeanor was truly angelic and Mrs. Bowden recalled seeing this behavior only from elementary girls about to receive first communion. Mrs. Bowden suspected the girls were behaving this way for her, but she appreciated the gesture just the same.

The Mass started when Jack began to play. He looked out over the crowd and watched as everyone sang. Jack turned to Father Joseph who smiled from behind the altar. The power of his music moved his classmates. He looked out from his elevated position over the students and listened to them sing to his music with happiness in their voices. He had never been more proud. The student body, who had only known him as a "football hero", was finally able to see another side of him.

When Mass ended, Jack's mother and brother came up to the front to greet him.

Mrs. Bowden gave him a big hug and praised him to the point of exaggeration. "That was the best Mass I've ever attended. You were incredible. That was the best you've ever played. I can't wait until next week."

"Thanks, Mom," Jack said, trying to be modest.

"Oh, I loved it. This was far better than any football game."

"Mom, you remember my friends, Tim, Ken and Mark?"

"Oh, yes. You young men look very nice. You are all so handsome in your jackets and ties. I wish you dressed this nice all of the time," Mrs. Bowden said, having seen the boys at her house numerous times dressed like hobos.

The three boys smiled but didn't say anything.

"Mom, this is Jenna, Victoria, and Hannah."

"It's so nice to meet you Mrs. Bowden," Jenna said, speaking for all three girls.

"You girls are so pretty in your uniforms. I believe Jack has spoken of you before," Mrs. Bowden revealed to Jenna.

Inside, Jenna was excited to hear this news but remained calm on the outside. "Jack's some musician, isn't he?" Jenna said, making Mrs. Bowden even more proud.

"Yes, he is," agreed Mrs. Bowden, raising her arms for another hug from her eldest son.

Suddenly, out of the departing crowd, Wendy appeared. She brushed right past Mrs. Bowden and Jack's friends. "Wow! Jack, that was terrific. I didn't know you were that good."

"Thanks, Wendy. I didn't see you during Mass," Jack said, wanting to know where she was sitting.

"I was late as usual and I had to sit in the back," Wendy announced to the throng of onlookers.

"That's too bad," Jack said sympathetically.

"Oh well, I've got to go," Wendy remarked as she placed Jack's keys in his hand. "I'll meet you after the game." She kissed him on the cheek and left without a word to the others.

While Jack's blood pumped with anticipation, his mother's blood boiled from aggravation.

Chapter 4

"Mom, have you seen my cleats?" Jack yelled down the hall. "I've got to go and I can't find my cleats."

"Have you checked the closet?" his mother asked in response to his question.

"No."

"Well, check the closet."

"I found them."

"That's good."

"Mom, have you seen my football jersey?"

"Jack, did you check the laundry?"

"Clean or dirty?"

"The dryer, I think."

"I found it."

Sam just waited patiently in the car. This conversation was common place on game day. It seemed like Jack could never find anything when it was time to go. It wasn't as if he couldn't find things on any other day. It was always on game day. Jack's mind was so consumed with taking on blockers and tackling ball carriers, that his mind went numb to the challenges of assembling his gear.

Jack opened the trunk and threw his bag in the back.

Opening the front door to the car, Jack moved into the driver's seat.

"You got everything?" Sam jested.

"Shut up!" Jack snorted, wiping the sweat from his brow.

*

The temperature hovered around sixty degrees as the purple sky dimmed with the setting sun. St. Mary's stadium was overflowing with people. The band played and crowd hummed as the announcer came over the public address system.

"Welcome to tonight's game between East Greenwich and Sacred Heart. Now entering the stadium are the East Greenwich Avengers." With that, the East Greenwich team took the field to a roar from the visiting crowd.

While waiting for the announcer to call his team into the stadium, Jack stood with Coach Dawson at the front of the line. He had played a hundred football games and he always felt the same. He was full of nervous energy. He bounced on his toes while his stomach churned. The game was the same but the year was different. Everyone on the team expected to Jack to lead them to victory and he was determined to do just that.

Jack checked his equipment a final time. Seeing the number fifty-one on his jersey, he recalled the glory days of a year ago. His team had often compared him to the infamous Dick Butkus because he hit opponents in the same bone crushing style.

Flashing back to the East Greenwich game the previous year, Jack remembered blocking on a punt return. Out of position, he couldn't block in front of the ball carrier, so he peeled back to block the defenders giving chase. At full speed, he blindsided his target. He hit the would-be tackler so hard; he lifted him up and drove him into a second defender taking both players to the ground. The coaches and players talked about that particular block the rest of the season. His buddies subsequently nicknamed him 'The Jack Hammer'. Now, it was a year later and he was preparing to build upon his reputation.

The team pulled together and Coach Dawson gave his players a few final words. "I want you to go out there and give it your best. Don't hold anything back. I want you to play like it's the last game you'll ever play."

With that, the Screaming Eagles ran onto the field through a gauntlet of supporters. Jack broke through the huge banner the cheerleaders held and the rest of the team followed.

Once on the sideline, the players fidgeted and moved about trying to calm their nerves. Jack, Chuck, and Matt jogged to the center of the field for the coin flip.

"I'm calling the coin toss," Chuck said as a matter of fact.

"Why do you get to call it?" Matt asked, only because Chuck made it seem important.

"Because I'm the quarterback," Chuck reasoned.

"So? I'm the tailback and I can kick your butt," Matt argued.

"Shut up! Both of you," Jack ordered.

Chuck and Matt obeyed.

They shook hands with the East Greenwich captains and the official asked Chuck to call it in the air.

"Heads," called Chuck and Matt at the same time.

"It's tails," the official announced.

"Nice call, knucklehead," Jack said aloud, shaking his head.

"Who are you calling knucklehead?" Chuck wanted to know.

49

"Both of you," Jack said, regretting his association with either of them.

After the opening kickoff, the Sacred Heart defense took the field. The defense huddled on the ball. Mark, Tim, Jack, and Ken put their hands out on top of each other's and the rest of the unit joined in.

"This is it, gentlemen. When you stick, stick hard. Don't stop moving until the whistle blows," Jack ordered. Then he called the play. "Zone coverage, 3-4 on the ball. Ready, break."

Jack lined up just behind Ken who played defensive tackle in the scheme. Keying on the tight end, Jack looked for him to block down on Ken for a running play.

East Greenwich lined up in an I formation. As the quarterback called the signals, the wide receiver went into motion. The quarterback took the ball from the center and handed it to the tailback. The right guard charged Jack and the ball carrier dodged to the outside. Jack took the guard straight up and threw him down. Both Ken and Jack met the ball carrier simultaneously. They drove him backward and then landed on him. Ken and Jack celebrated their stop while the running back lay beneath them. East Greenwich lost two yards on the play.

Expecting a pass on second and twelve, Jack called the next play, "Man coverage, 4-3 slant, Mike blitz."

The East Greenwich quarterback dropped back to pass. The blocking broke down under heavy pressure. The quarterback stepped up and Tim hit him from behind. The Avengers lost ten more yards.

Exhilaration radiated from the Screaming Eagles' huddle.

"Did you see that? The blocking crumbled!" Mark shouted.

"Let's stick it to them. Attack the ball!" Tim chimed in.

"Okay, settle down, one play to go," Jack said, trying to calm his exuberant defense. "On me. On me. It's third and 22. Stunt four deep zone. Stunt four deep zone," he repeated.

The East Greenwich offense came out in a spread formation. Sure enough, as Jack anticipated, the quarterback dropped back to pass and threw a deep ball up the sideline. Mark came over to double the receiver and knocked the ball away.

"Three and out! Three and out!" Mark shouted again and again, pumping his fist. He sprinted to the sideline and received a series of head butts and handshakes from his teammates.

Jack sneaked a peak at the cheerleaders and Wendy blew him a kiss. He then looked up in the stands to find his parents. They were in their customary spot. Jack's father gave him a wave and he returned the gesture.

Coach Dawson was too busy giving instructions to the offense to congratulate his defense. Sacred Heart had the ball on the East Greenwich forty-eight and Coach Dawson wanted to score on their first possession. He sent in a series of pass plays for a quick strike.

Cruise dropped back to pass on first down and hit Willie Shaffer on a crossing pattern for fifteen yards. On the second play, Cruise hooked up with John Tanner for another twenty-two yards. Then, with the ball on the eleven yard line, Cruise dropped back to pass and then with the receivers covered, he scrambled up the middle for a touchdown. Sacred Heart kicked the point after and led 7-0.

Back on the field for the second time, Jack and the defense stymied the Avenger offense. First, the Avengers ran off left tackle and Jack was there to stuff the hole. Then it was a sweep to the right. Jack took out the lead blocker and Mark pushed the tailback down on his way out of bounds. On third down, Jack blitzed up the middle and met Ken at the quarterback for another sack.

The pattern repeated over and over. The half came and Sacred Heart was dominating 21-0. Cruise had thrown two touchdown passes and had run for one. The Screaming Eagles were also overpowering on defense. They had given up only three first downs and hadn't allowed the Avengers to cross midfield.

Sam accompanied Jack to the locker room.

"You look unstoppable out there," Sam complimented.

"Yeah, we're kicking butt. But they aren't that good," Jack retorted as they jogged up the runway.

"What are you planning for the second half?" Sam asked Jack.

"We'll back off a bit. We'll play it conservative and not give up any big plays."

"Not us," Cruise interrupted. "We're gonna run it up!"

"We'll see," Jack countered, knowing full well that the coaches called the offensive plays.

The Screaming Eagles took the first possession of the second half. Just as Cruise had said, the Screaming Eagles came out throwing. Cruise used play action to hold the linebackers and hit pass after pass. On one stretch, he hit seven consecutive passes. Cruise and the offense scored at will and led heading into the fourth quarter, 35-0.

Coach Dawson had seen enough. He called Cruise over for a conference.

"What's up, Coach?" Cruise asked.

"The game's over. We're going to run out the clock," Coach Dawson said, assessing his team's field position.

"Come on, Coach! We only need seven more points," Cruise argued.

"Seven more points for what?" Coach Dawson replied, somewhat suspicious.

"Ah...ah, we need seven more points because I promised my little sister I would throw five touchdown passes tonight and I've only thrown four," Cruise lied.

"You're kidding, right? You really don't expect me to let you run up the score because of a promise you made to your little sister. She's not sick in the hospital is she?" Dawson asked.

Cruise knew better than to push his luck and shook his head no.

"Just run out the clock," Coach Dawson ordered.

Cruise knelt in the huddle. "Coach said to run out the clock. But he didn't say we couldn't score doing it. Thirty-four dive on two." Cruise turned to Singleton and said, "Matt, I need another touchdown."

Play after play, the Screaming Eagles ran the ball down the Avengers' throats. Chewing up the field, three, four and five yards at a time, the Screaming Eagles worked the ball down to the East Greenwich twelve yard line. In doing so, the clock had run down to eighteen seconds.

Again, Cruise knelt in the middle of the huddle. "We only have time for one more play. We didn't drive the whole field to just lie down and quit. He looked at each face in the huddle for concurrence and then said, "Split end reverse on two."

"Coach Dawson said to run out the clock," Singleton argued before the break. "He's gonna kill you. He'll probably kill all of us."

"You're either with me or against me. What's it going to be?" Cruise demanded.

No one spoke a word.

"Okay, let's put the nail in the coffin," Cruise barked.

Cruise took the snap and handed off to Singleton. Singleton swept right and gave it to Tanner, coming back to the left. With the entire line moving to the right, Cruise was Tanner's only blocker. First, Cruise cut the defensive end to the ground and then rebounded to kick out the safety. Tanner scored easily thanks to Cruise's devastating blocks.

Coach Dawson went after Cruise like a man possessed. "What the hell was that?"

"You said to run out the clock and that's what we did. You can't fault the offense for playing hard."

"I can't tell if you're dumb or just stupid, Cruise. We'll find out on Monday at practice," Coach Dawson said, gritting his teeth.

*

Wendy and Jack sat on the hood of Jack's car. Parked on the deserted Oakland Beach, the couple could see the waves crashing on the beach by the September moonlight.

"This is so romantic, Jack. I love the ocean. It makes me feel so alive."

"Yeah, this is great," Jack agreed as leaned over to kiss Wendy.

"What did you think of tonight's game?" Jack asked, needing some recognition for his play.

"The crowd was pretty loud until halftime. They lost interest after that. It must have had something to do with the score," Wendy remarked. "Our routines went pretty well," Wendy added about her own performance.

"What about the game? What did you think of the game?" Jack questioned with his lips inches from Wendy's.

"You know I don't know anything about football," Wendy said, giving him a kiss between each word she spoke. Then she added, "Your butt looks real tight in those little pants," as she ran her hand up Jack's thigh.

Clearly distracted, Jack pulled Wendy on top of him and ran his hands over her firm body. Jack's heart raced when Wendy eased her tongue deep in his mouth.

"Jack," Wendy whispered.

"Yes," Jack answered, knowing by heart the conversation that was to follow.

"You know I'm in love with you, and you know I want to please you....I don't want to spoil things when they are going so well," Wendy pleaded.

"I know... I know. But when? Surely, you don't expect me to wait until we're married."

This didn't shock Wendy at all. They had spoken of marriage quite often during their year long relationship. Jack agreed to almost anything in the heat of passion.

"No, Jack, I don't. How about we wait until Homecoming? My parents will be out of town that weekend and then we can totally enjoy ourselves."

Hearing those words were music to his ears. Jack leapt off the car and yelled to the deserted beach, "I'm the happiest man in the entire world!" Then he thrust his fists in the air, "This is truly the greatest day of my life!"

Wendy became embarrassed and ran after Jack. When Wendy came at him at full speed, Jack turned away from her. She jumped on his back, knocking him off his feet. The two tumbled into the sand. Jack turned over and Wendy sat on his chest.

"I love you Jack Bowden. And this is not the greatest day of your life. Homecoming will be the greatest day of your life. I guarantee it."

Wendy swiveled her hips stoking Jack's fire.

Jack rolled Wendy onto her back and they made out like bandits.

*

"Thank you, Mrs. Bowden," Ken said, taking another bowl of popcorn from Jack's mother. "It sure is nice of you to fix all these snacks for us."

"You're welcome. I hope you boys are having a good time," Mrs. Bowen said as she cleaned up a few dishes before heading up the stairs.

"Hey Jack, what's up with Wendy and your mother? I thought they were going to go at it yesterday in church," Ken stated, wanting details.

"What?" Jack asked with a grin. "Oh, that. Yeah, Wendy and my mother are having this thing. I can't get in the middle of it so I'm trying to keep them apart."

"It's not working," Sam piped in. "Mom hates her."

"That's obvious," Ken confirmed.

"How's it going with Wendy? Are you guys getting serious?" Tim inquired with peaked interest.

"Shut up with the girl talk! Let's get down to business," Jack said, trying to change the subject.

"How about Wendy? She's such a babe," Ken digressed.

"Did you see her in her cheerleading uniform last night? Unbelievable," Tim said, answering his own question.

"Hey, you know what I heard last night after the game?" Ken asked everyone in general but no one in particular. "I heard from Victoria that Jenna is in love with Jack."

"That's just wrong." Tim frowned. "Jack gets all the babes."

Taking another handful of popcorn, Ken explained, "He's just a freakin' chick magnet."

All the boys laughed except for Jack who stopped to reflect upon the two girls. He liked both Wendy and Jenna. Both girls were very attractive. Sure, Wendy was a little pushy and Jenna seemed nicer. But he had a lot of time invested with Wendy and things were looking real good for Homecoming.

"I don't have time for this," Jack said, calming the ruckus. "Can we please watch the video?"

The boys turned their attention to the game film of Pilgrim and Cranston East.

"Play that back again," Tim instructed.

Sam pushed two buttons on the remote and the group of boys watched Pilgrim score a touchdown for a second time.

"Did you see that?" Mark asked, pointing to the receiver. "He broke off his pattern over the middle when he read blitz. The quarterback didn't even hesitate. It must have been a designed option. Holy hell! These guys are going to be tough."

The defense sat crowded in a tiny room in the Bowden's basement as Sam showed them play after play of Pilgrim's 34-6 win over Cranston East.

When the first showing ended, Ken asked Sam in utter amazement. "How in the heck did you get their film so fast? They just beat East last night."

"It was nothing," Sam answered, trying to be modest. "My friend Mike Kersey recorded the game. We cataloged each play sequentially and by situation. So if you want to watch the game as it happened, you can. Or if you want to see the play selection by down, you can do that, too."

"We're going to kick their butts!" Ken hollered.

"Easy Ken," Jack interrupted. "It's not that simple. Sam, can you explain to them what you told me earlier?"

"Sure. We can usually tell what play they will run from the formation. But in most of their formations, they have options built into the play."

"So…most offenses do that. That's nothing new." Tim countered.

"But Pilgrim's options are better than most. Let me give you an example," Sam said as he keyed up another play from the East game. "Here's a play where they line up in a split backfield on second down. In this particular play, there is no blitz and the pressure is minimal. The quarterback throws deep over the middle for twenty-two yards."

Pushing some more buttons, Sam brought up another play. "The situation here is similar. It is second down and again a split backfield. This time the pass rush is effective and the QB dumps the ball into the flat with a receiver coming out of the backfield. This play goes for twenty-eight yards and a touchdown."

Ken seemed dumbfounded. "So… now what?"

Jack stood in front of the screen to capture their undivided attention. "The good news is we know all of their plays. We know what players touch the ball and from what formations. We stand a good chance of getting lucky at least a couple of times. Maybe we'll be able to intercept a pass or make a key stop on third down. Sam is going to be on the sidelines with all of their plays and formations mapped out. He's going to signal us with what he thinks is coming."

Chapter 5

Victoria whispered into Tim's ear, "Didn't I tell you Jenna was in love with Jack? Look at her. She's all over him."

Tim shook his head in agreement. "I think he likes her, too. If they ever get together, you want to double with them?"

"Are you asking me out on a date?" Victoria deduced. "I don't want to wait for them. You can take me to the party after the game this Friday."

"Wow! That was easy," Tim said, expressing relief.

"Getting the date may be easy, but I'm certainly not. You'd better not try anything funny," Victoria warned.

Victoria and Tim retrieved their chemicals and walked back to the lab table where Jack and Jenna were setting up their equipment for the experiment.

Jenna tried to push the glass tubing through the rubber stopper while Jack rigged the flask to the ring stand clamp.

"Am I doing this right?" Jenna asked Jack.

"As if I know," Jack teased before taking the stopper from Jenna. "You have to put some glycerin on the glass so it will slide through the stopper."

"Thank you, Jack," Jenna said watching him work the stopper.

"Are you ready for the hydrochloric acid?" Tim asked as he approached the lab table.

"Not quite. Why don't you two go ahead and measure the chemicals while we finish setting up," Jack suggested to Victoria and Tim.

The four students worked vigorously to get the experiment started. Once the chemicals were mixed, the group sat back and relaxed while the chemicals reacted.

"You guys played great Friday," Jenna remarked out of the silence.

"Yeah, we killed," Tim reminisced.

"You were there?" Jack asked, taking interest in Jenna's attendance.

"Sure. Vic, Sarah and I all went," Jenna answered.

Jenna stared deep into Jack's eyes. "You played an awesome game. I must have seen you make twelve tackles. I remember right before the half, East Greenwich ran a sweep to the side we were sitting on and you knocked the runner down going out of bounds. It was so loud, I thought the guy was going to need an ambulance."

"That's so cool that you actually watched me play," Jack said, appreciating the compliments.

Jack was drawn to Jenna. Somebody finally gave him the recognition he had so desired. Sure, his parents and brother always praised him for his accomplishments, but even the coaches and players were indirect with their appreciation.

"Man, that was some wild hit, I thought that guy was dead," Tim added. Then motioning toward Jack, Tim remarked, "We don't call him the 'The Hammer' for nothing."

"Hammer?" Jenna questioned with a confused expression.

"Yeah. That's his nickname. Hammer. It's short for 'Jack Hammer' because he hits so hard."

The girls started laughing.

"Hey, Hammer. Can you give me a hand with these nails?" Victoria teased causing Jenna to laugh with her.

"Hey, Tim. Can you help me hang a few pictures? Make sure you bring the Hammer," Victoria giggled, creating a greater ruckus.

Jenna composed herself quickly when Jack only slightly smiled.

"Well, you played an outstanding game, Hammer. You don't mind if I call you Hammer, do you?"

"No, I guess not," Jack said, hoping this wouldn't get back to Wendy. Wendy would go insane if she heard another girl call him by a nickname that hardly anyone knew outside of the football team. Jack then wondered if Wendy was even aware of his nickname.

"So, Jenna, you like football?" Jack asked, wanting to extend the conversation in his area of expertise.

"Sure, who doesn't like football?" Jenna replied as Victoria raised her hand. "My dad played college football at Nebraska State. My whole life has revolved around football. We even went to the Sugar Bowl last year."

Thoroughly impressed, Jack hung on every word Jenna said the rest of the period.

*

The football team was going through its normal routine of stretching and conditioning. The mood was light and players were loose following their easy victory over East Greenwich.

"Chuck, get over here!" ordered Coach Dawson.

Cruise grabbed his helmet and jogged over to where Coach Dawson and Coach Williams were standing.

"Yeah, Coach?" Cruise mumbled, remembering how upset Coach Dawson was after Friday's game.

"Recall when I told you to run out the clock and you pulled that reverse on the last play? I'm still pissed about that. The East Greenwich coach is really angry and he *was* a friend of mine. He thinks I was trying to run up the score," Coach Dawson lectured. "I'm going to split time between you and Walters at quarterback during practice. If you pull anything like that again, I'll send Walters in quicker than you can scratch your head."

"C'mon Coach. Walters couldn't lead this team to the shower room much less the end zone. I know it was wrong. It'll never happen again," Cruise pleaded.

Coach Dawson knew Cruise was right about Walters. But, he needed to make Cruise believe it was possible he would lose his starting position.

"If it does, you'll never step foot on the playing field again," Coach Dawson barked.

Coach Dawson blew his whistle and shouted, "Offense over here. Defense, go with Coach Williams."

Sam always hated this part of practice. His brother and friends migrated across the field leaving him with Cruise, Hamilton, and Singleton.

"First team on the ball," Coach Dawson shouted.

After the starting unit stepped up to the ball, Coach Dawson called the play, "X curl, Z out."

Cruise stepped up behind the center imagining there was a defensive team on the opposite side of the line. "On two, on two. Hut one, hut two."

The center hiked the ball and Cruise dropped back to pass. The linemen formed a pocket simulating a defensive pass rush. Tanner faked inside and cut out. Cruise anticipated the cut and threw before Tanner looked. When Tanner turned, the ball met his hands with perfect velocity. Tanner grasped the ball and turned up field before coming to a stop and returning to the original line of scrimmage. Tanner promptly tossed the football back to the center.

"Again, but this time, hit Summers on the curl," Coach Dawson demanded, looking at his clipboard.

Again, Cruise took the ball and again, he delivered it with pinpoint accuracy.

Coach Dawson turned to Walters and said, "Your turn."

Despite being informed earlier that he would share quarterbacking duties during practice, Buck Walter's limp body bristled in shock. Not having played the preceding year, Walters, a sophomore, had not even taken a single snap in three weeks of practice.

Walters was a meek boy that didn't have many skills. He earned the job as second string quarterback by default. Upperclassmen were aware of Cruise's talent and stature at quarterback and concluded their playing time would be severely limited if they volunteered to be his backup.

Strapping on his helmet, Walters ran onto the field. On the first play, he fumbled the snap from center and the offense had to reset. On the second play, hesitation in his voice caused the left side of the line to move early.

The more plays Walters ran, the more dysfunctional he became. His first pass sailed over the receiver's outstretched arms. His second pass hit a lineman in the head. The third pass slipped out of his hand when he brought his arm forward.

The offense complained of his incompetence.

"C'mon you loser!" shouted Hamilton. "Can't you do anything right?"

"I'm not running a long pattern until he can hit the short ones," Tanner whined.

Cruise stood on the sidelines and enjoyed the revolt almost as much as he did the errant passing of his backup. "C'mon Walters, show us what you're made of," Cruise taunted.

Walters ran six more unsuccessful plays before Coach Dawson called an end to the fiasco.

Coach Dawson blew his whistle and the entire team assembled for a scrimmage.

The offense had no idea what was about to happen. They casually took the field with the ball on the twenty yard line. When they broke the huddle, Sam quickly assessed the formation from the sideline. With both Jack and Mark looking, Sam signaled by raising his right foot that the offense was running to the right.

Jack and Mark both moved to their left, anticipating the direction of the play. After Cruise took the ball from the center, he pitched the ball to Singleton. Jack and Mark penetrated the back field and were on top of him before he had a chance to turn up field. They tackled him for a six yard loss.

Without celebration, the defenders huddled. Once in the huddle, however, Jack and his friends laughed heartily.

"This is like shooting fish in a barrel," Ken chuckled, enjoying their success.

"I can't wait until they start passing," Tim remarked, wanting a shot at Cruise.

"When they pass, we go man to man. Everyone else blitz," Jack stated as a matter of fact. "You know their routes. Cover the short ones because they aren't going to have time for a long pass. Step in front and make the interception. Everyone watch Sam for the signal. And remember, no high fives, no celebration. They'll know something is up."

The offense came quietly to the line. Sam raised his right hand. The pass play had been called. The defense hid their blitz by keeping everyone in a standard set. But when the ball was snapped, eight defenders charged through the line.

Four defenders broke through clean and knocked Cruise to the ground. The defensive players helped Cruise to his feet, pretending to be good sports.

Back in the huddle, the defense was having a party.

"Who got him first?" Mark asked.

Tim pointed at Jack, "The Hammer crushed him."

From the sideline, Sam could see the defensive huddle shaking as the boys' bodies convulsed with laughter.

"Same play," Jack snickered.

Again, Sam raised his right arm to signal a pass. The defense inched forward ready for another onslaught. When the ball was snapped, the defense sprinted across the line. They attacked from all directions. The pocket crumbled like day old bread. Within moments, Cruise was buried under a pile of humanity.

After the defenders got up, Cruise staggered to his feet. "What the hell?" he cried. He threw his arms in the air. "I can't throw if I don't have time to look."

The offensive line was overwhelmed. They could only block one person each.

"It seems like they're playing with twelve or thirteen players," Hamilton grumbled.

"Shut up and block somebody, you idiot!" Singleton said, airing his frustration to the limitless excuses. "Just throw the short pass, will you?"

When the offense lined up, Jack could see the next play before Sam even gave the sign. Again, in a standard set, the linebackers dropped back on the next pass. Jack waited for Tanner to make his cut across the middle and stepped in front of him as the ball was being delivered. Jack caught the ball on the run and raced toward the goal line around the right end. Cruise chased him down but was no match for his strength. Slowing down, Jack stiff armed Cruise in the face and drove him to the ground. He then jogged the rest of the way to the end zone for a touchdown.

Walking back to the scrimmage line, Jack tossed the ball to Cruise and taunted, "Nice tackle."

Cruise walked over to the sideline. He mysteriously developed a limp that worsened when he approached Coach Dawson. After a few moments with Cruise, Coach Dawson turned to Walters and said, "You're in."

Jack looked over at Sam. While Sam was in uniform, his arm was still recovering from the dislocation that he suffered only a week ago.

"Okay, you guys, nobody hits Walters. Back off on the pass rush and give him time. We can't afford to have him get hurt," Jack reasoned. "Besides, he needs the practice."

Nodding in agreement, the defense played straight even though they knew what was coming. Although Walters was given time, he still proved incompetent. He failed to complete any passes and fumbled twice handing the ball off.

"That's enough for today," Coach Dawson said in frustration. "See you tomorrow at the same time."

Walking off the field, Coach Dawson approached Jack.

"You guys really put it on Cruise today, huh?"

"Yeah," Jack agreed modestly.

"It was fun to watch," Coach Dawson said, evoking a grin from Jack. "Let's not do it again."

Jack laughed before responding, "You're the coach."

Coach Dawson put his arm around Jack and they walked in together.

*

Ms. Thomas finished her discussion regarding the assignment and directed the students to form their groups. Wendy, Jack, Kelly, and Matt moved their desks together. Jack didn't particularly care for being in the same group as Matt but Wendy insisted. Her best friend, Kelly, was dating Matt and it made their English group seem more like a double date than a work group.

"I love it when Ms. Thomas has us do small group discussion. It makes it so much easier for me to understand the book," Wendy confessed to the trio facing her.

Poking fun at her, Jack quipped, "It'd help if you actually read the book."

"Not laughing," Wendy grumbled, "That's not very nice."

"Let's get started," Matt suggested.

"Yes, let's see," Kelly agreed and read from her paper. "What is the relationship between Captain Ahab and Moby Dick?"

"That's easy," proclaimed Wendy. "Captain Ahab is the fisherman and Moby Dick is the fish."

"Moby Dick is a whale, not a fish," Matt corrected.

"Whale, fish, what's the big deal?" Wendy countered, then added, "Why is the whale named Moby Dick anyway? I hate saying 'dick'. I find it offensive."

"Have you ever seen a whale's penis?" Matt inquired, realizing the unlikelihood she had.

"That's just gross!" Kelly exclaimed, punching Matt in the chest for bringing it up.

"No, really. The sperm whale has the largest penis of any animal in the world," Matt said, trying to defend himself. "It's like five feet long. I saw it at a museum in New Bedford."

Becoming embarrassed, Kelly frowned. "Shut up."

Laughing, Jack turned to Matt and said, "You know who's a real dick? Cruise. How can you hang out with the guy? He's so uncool."

Kelly and Wendy suddenly became very interested in what Jack had to say. Jack rarely participated in gossip or judged someone so negatively.

"He's okay," Matt answered without conviction.

"Ya think? You saw what he did to my brother, and what about that reverse he called on the last play leading 35-0? And that's just been the past two weeks," Jack argued.

"I won't talk about him. He's just been acting weird lately," Matt defended.

"How did you guys ever become friends in the first place? You're so different," Wendy asked, putting life back into the conversation.

"His uncle married my cousin when we were in the third grade. Since we lived close by, we seemed to see each other at every family function," Matt explained.

"That's too bad," Jack sympathized.

"What's too bad?" Matt wondered.

"That you're related to a dick," Jack mused.

Chapter 6

The Screaming Eagles traveled across town to play the Pilgrim Patriots. Directly prior to the opening kickoff, the defense huddled around Sam for a final review of the signals. Sam had made a set of colored cards and instructed the defense on the meaning of each.

"Red means run. If it's in my right hand, they'll run right. Left hand means run left. If I hold it in the middle of my body like this, it means up the middle. The green card means pass. If I hold it up over my head, it means long pass. At the belt means, short pass," Sam detailed, moving the cards around his body. "You have to remember that this is just a probability. It's not a sure thing."

Jumping in, Jack added, "I don't want anyone looking at Sam besides Mark and myself. If nine of us are playing straight, we won't get sucked into an option. Be aggressive and listen for audibles."

The defense took the field first and readied for the first play. Pilgrim lined up at their own thirty-five. Sam assessed the formation and consulted the clipboard. Seeing the wide receiver line up on the narrow side of the field with a wishbone backfield, Sam could easily see an option play coming right. Sam held the red card in his outstretched right hand. Mark and Jack both identified the formation and agreed with Sam's assessment. They both crept forward to their left. The quarterback moved to his right with the ball. With the fullback option unavailable, he faked the handoff and moved around the right end. Jack covered the quarterback and Mark spied the pitchman. The quarterback could see the pitch was covered and opted to carry it himself. The quarterback attempted to bring it back to the middle but Jack met him at the line of scrimmage and wrestled him to the ground for no gain.

On second and ten, Pilgrim called a deep crossing route. On Sam's signal, Mark hung back and doubled the primary receiver, while the defense rushed five. Jack gave the tailback some space in the flat so the quarterback would throw to him once he saw the pressure. The quarterback did just as Jack had predicted. He paused after looking over the middle and lofted a pass into the flat. Jack timed his break on the ball perfectly. He snared the ball a split second before it reached the receiver. Catching the ball in full stride, Jack took the ball back thirty-two yards for a touchdown.

Returning to the sideline, the Screaming Eagles' defense jumped on Jack, knocking him to the ground. Jack got up and high fived his brother. The kick was good and Sacred Heart led 7-0.

After the ensuing kickoff, the defense was on the field again. Jack and Mark glanced over to Sam before each down and anticipated every play. Pilgrim lost three yards on first down and another five on second down. On third and eighteen, Pilgrim threw a post pattern pass. This time Mark stepped in front of the receiver and intercepted the pass. Mark headed down the sidelines for a second defensive touchdown and a 14-0 lead.

Amidst a second celebration, Cruise and the offense became envious. Sacred Heart was beating Pilgrim High 14-0 and the offense had not run a play. Pilgrim was regarded by many as an elite team and was supposed to be a big hurdle for the Screaming Eagles.

"Alright, alright! Way to go D," Cruise said half-heartedly, wishing he were the one scoring the touchdowns. Then he noticed the defense congratulating Sam.

"Hey, Matt. What's that all about? Why would they be yucking it up with the third string quarterback?"

"I don't know. Why don't you go ask them?" suggested Singleton.

Cruise walked over to Sam who was preparing himself for the next defensive series. "What are you doing?" Cruise asked with contempt for Sam.

"Nothing," Sam responded.

"What's that in your hand?" Cruise demanded to know.

"It's a clipboard. What does it look like?" Sam replied, turning it away from Cruise so he couldn't read it.

Cruise continued his interrogation, "What are those colored cards for?"

"None of your business."

By now, Sam had memorized all of Pilgrim's sets and signaled the plays without consulting the clipboard.

Cruise, who refused to retreat, watched as Sam signaled the defense. Cruise then witnessed the defense make adjustments prior to defeating the offensive plays. The defense moved to the left to wipe out a sweep by Pilgrim on first down. On second down, Cruise observed the defense stop a Pilgrim run up the middle. On third down, the Pilgrim quarterback pitched wild and Mark picked up the fumble, scoring his second touchdown of the game.

"What's going on here?" Cruise shouted, grabbing Sam by the jersey. "How do you know their plays?"

"None of your business," Sam answered as Cruise lifted him up onto his toes.

Jack saw Cruise jerk his brother around as he jogged to the sidelines. "What the hell do you think you're doing?" Jack asked, pushing Cruise away from Sam.

Cruise regained his balance and approached Jack in a sudden and threatening manner. "You guys are cheating. I saw it. Sam is signaling you their plays. That's cheating."

Pushing Cruise, Jack shot back, "It's not cheating, you dickhead!"

Finally, with two minutes to go in the first quarter, the offense got on the field with the Screaming Eagles leading 21-0.

At halftime, Jack and the defense were in a festive mood. Pilgrim had only gotten one first down and the defense had scored three touchdowns.

"We're killing 'em!" Tim bellowed.

"Give me some of that," Mark hollered, holding out his hand for Tim to slap.

The boys spun around getting fives from all sides.

"Jack, can I see you and Sam in my office?" interrupted Coach Dawson.

Sam could already see Cruise in the office through the glass before they walked in.

"Chuck says you guys are cheating and that's why we're winning so easily. He says Sam knows their plays and signals them into you," Coach Dawson said to Jack.

"And that's cheating how?" Jack asked

"If you stole their playbook or something like that?" Coach Dawson explained.

"We didn't steal anything," Jack protested.

Sam didn't want the cat to get out of the bag. If the other teams knew they could learn so much from studying film, they would change their plays or even start studying film themselves.

Before Jack could come clean with the truth, Sam's voice cracked, "I'm psychic. I can tell what play they will run right before it happens."

Coach Dawson, Jack, and Cruise looked at Sam.

"Psychic, huh?" Coach Dawson chuckled knowing full well that was a lie. The truth was Coach Dawson didn't want the truth. He wanted a state championship. "Well good for you…good for us. Keep up the good work. Now, all three of you, get out of my office."

Cruise's mouth dropped open when he heard Coach Dawson's reaction. Jack and Sam, on the other hand, held their collective breaths as they departed, hoping the truth wouldn't somehow escape.

The Screaming Eagles' defense dominated play in the second half and Sacred Heart won the game 28-0.

*

Opening the passenger door, Jack helped Wendy out of his car. They walked up to Tim's house holding hands. The brightly illuminated house was the site of the post-game party. Loud music pounded their hearts as they approached the front door. Wendy reached for the doorbell, but Jack went ahead and turned the knob sensing that the doorbell would go unheard.

The front room was crowded with schoolmates. Some stood in small groups telling stories while others danced in the middle of the room. Jack and Wendy weaved through the people looking for familiar faces. The couple's appearance was greeted with compliments on Jack's play and Wendy's outfit. They made their way into the kitchen where Jack found most of his buddies toasting their victory.

"Here's to us!" Tim shouted, raising his plastic cup high into the air.

"To us!" the others repeated.

"Nice to see you made it, Jack," Tim said cheerfully before he saw Wendy. Then he glumly added, "Hi Wendy, good to see you, too."

"Some party," Jack noted over the music, "Are your parents home?"

"No. They're out of town for the night. Want something to drink?"

"Sure," Jack said, taking one for himself and while handing the other to Wendy.

The boys lost their enthusiasm to party with Wendy hovering over them. Feeling the tension, Wendy left Jack to find her own friends. With Wendy gone, the guys started replaying the game.

"Hey, Jack, that was a great game we played, huh?" Ken said, congratulating the whole defense. "How about the way you baited the quarterback to throw into the flat? Then you intercepted the pass as if it were intended for you the whole time."

"Yeah, it was great." Jack confirmed, while looking in the direction of Wendy, who had wandered into the next room.

Each player took a turn recounting the key plays in which they participated. After each play was described, the team would toast the players involved. When it was Jack's turn in the circle, he gave credit to his brother.

"Here's to Sam!" Jack shouted. "We're lucky to have him on our side."

With that, all the smiling faces went straight. After a moment of deep reflection about Sam's contribution, Tim broke the silence and raised his glass, "Here, here...here's to Sam, a little brother to all of us."

"Where is the third stringer anyway?" Mark asked.

"He's at home prepping the Toll Gate film," Jack snickered, thinking ahead to next week's game.

"You're kidding," Tim said, knowing it was probably true. "You shouldn't work him so hard."

When the conversation shifted to their next opponent, Jack hoped their next game would be as easy. His attention was diverted when he saw Jenna following Victoria into the kitchen. Victoria went and stood next to Tim while Jenna approached Jack.

Wearing a black leather mini skirt with high heel boots, Jenna had Jack's full attention. She always looked good, but tonight, she was spectacular.

Jack gazed into her blue eyes and couldn't believe how attracted he was to her at this moment.

"Hey, Hammer! Nice game tonight."

Jack raised a finger to his lips and emitted an unintentionally loud, "Shhh." Not wanting Wendy to hear this exchange, he placed his hand over Jenna's mouth to keep her from repeating it.

Mark observed Jack's actions. Realizing what was happening, he pulled Jack away from Jenna. "What's the matter, Hammer? Afraid Wendy's going to get mad?"

"Shut up, will ya?" Jack begged.

"It's alright if she finds out. She's already mean to you," Mark whispered into Jack's ear.

"What's the matter?" Jenna asked Tim and Victoria.

"He's just a little embarrassed about the nickname," Tim fibbed.

Hearing this, the group of boys started singing MC Hammer's "Can't Touch This" above the already loud music coming from the next room. Victoria and Jenna began dancing to the chorus, which encouraged the boys to sing longer and louder.

The group began to chant, "Go Hammer, Go Hammer!" at which point Jenna danced over to Jack and put her arms around his neck while he leaned back against the kitchen counter. Jenna ran her arms down his torso making him tighten his abdomen. Jack watched as Jenna moved her hips back and forth in rhythm to the beat. While he didn't physically reciprocate, he most certainly enjoyed her affection.

Just as Jenna was giving Jack her best close in dance moves, Wendy walked into the kitchen. Wasting no time, Wendy grabbed Jack by the shoulder and twisted him away from Jenna.

"What are you doing?" she asked with rage in her voice. She pulled back her right hand and slapped Jack square in the face when he could offer no explanation. She walked out leaving him to feel the embarrassment alone.

Turning to face his friends and Jenna, Jack raised his glass one final time. "Thanks. Thanks a lot. I really enjoyed that. I'll be going now."

Jack walked out the door and followed Wendy to the street.

Once clear from the house, Jack called to her. "Wendy, please stop."

Wendy stopped and waited for Jack. When he caught up to her, he apologized. "I'm sorry. I didn't want that to happen. I'm real sorry," Jack said, putting his hand on her shoulder.

Shaking from the tears, Wendy spoke with sadness, "I feel so humiliated. I thought you loved me."

"I do love you, Wendy."

"Then why would you do that to me?"

"I didn't want it to happen. It just did," Jack offered sincerely. "I'm real sorry. Will you forgive me?"

Withholding her forgiveness, Wendy asked, "Why was Jenna dancing that way for you, anyway?"

"We're just friends. She was just having fun."

"I don't like her. She shouldn't be having that kind of fun with another girl's boyfriend, regardless of your friendship."

"I know," Jack agreed, hoping Wendy would end her hostility.

"I don't want you being friends with her anymore."

"But Wendy...c'mon. You can't expect me to stop talking to her just because we made a mistake."

Wendy thought for a minute and said, "I just don't want you being alone with her. Everyone can tell she's in love with you. Will you do that for me?"

"Yes, Wendy. I can do that."

"Thank you, Jack," Wendy said softly.

She put her arms around him and hugged him tight.

79

Chapter 7

Sitting with his guitar on his lap, Jack played for his own entertainment. He hammered his guitar with the power of a blacksmith. Masterfully, he moved his left hand up and down the neck, changing chords while maintaining the rhythm of the music.

He had spent many hours in the basement playing the music he loved, rock and roll. He had learned the music and the lyrics of many of his favorite rock artists and he especially enjoyed playing songs with sports themes. While his mother preferred religious tunes, his father and brother often sang along with him when they heard the upbeat music vibrate through the floor.

Queen, The Rolling Stones and Aerosmith were his favorites. His influence came from his father. Whenever the family would go on a road trip or just across town, Mr. Bowden had the radio tuned to the classic rock station. His mother and father would sing along with the radio trying to convince their sons they were cool. Consequently, Jack was turned on to this type of music because of his ability to understand and relate to the lyrics. Later on, he found that he enjoyed playing the songs on his guitar when it was nearly impossible to make sense of the music that most kids his age preferred.

"I can't get no...sat is faction. Hey, hey, hey. That's what I say," Jack sang, making his lips puff out to twice their normal size.

Jack was playing so loudly that he didn't hear the door to the basement open and his classmates come down the stairs. When he looked up from his music book, he saw Sam standing next to Tim, Mark, Ken, Victoria, Sarah and Jenna.

"Singing about Wendy again?" Tim said above the music to everyone's amusement.

Jack smiled but kept right on playing. The girls started doing their best '60s dance impressions and the boys joined in, singing the chorus. Jack finished with an extravagant ad-lib solo, much like a concert finale.

The moment the song ended, Jack asked with pleasant surprise, "What are you guys doing here tonight?"

"Study group!" Ken and Mark said together.

Jack saw the algebra books they were holding and quickly figured out Sam was tutoring his friends. But he asked anyway, "What are you studying?"

"Algebra," Mark answered, holding up his book so Jack could get a better look.

Noticing that Jenna didn't have a book, Jack remembered she wasn't taking algebra. "What are you studying, Jenna?"

"I'm not really part of the group. Vic told me she was coming over and I just wanted to see you."

Jack became excited on the inside but remained composed and somber on the outside.

"That's nice," Jack responded without breaking eye contact. "What did you want to see me about?"

"I just wanted to say how sorry I am for what happened Friday," Jenna lied, thinking about how wonderful she felt being so intimate with Jack even if only for a few seconds. "I certainly didn't mean to hurt you," she went on, trying to put some truth in her words. On the other hand, she really didn't mind if Wendy got hurt.

"That's okay, Wendy just overreacted. She didn't realize how close of friends we are. She's over it."

"I'm so relieved," Jenna said, suspecting otherwise.

It then became obvious to Jack that their conversation was disrupting the study group.

"We'll go upstairs," Jack announced to the group.

"Hey, Jack. Can you ask Mom if she'll make some snacks for us?" Sam asked, looking around at all of the hungry faces.

"Sure. See you guys later."

Jack and Jenna made their way up the stairs and into the kitchen where Mr. and Mrs. Bowden were sitting at the kitchen table.

"How's it going?" Mr. Bowden asked the couple.

"Pretty good. Do you mind if Jenna and I go into my room?" Jack asked and then explained, "Sam's group is studying and we didn't want to disturb them."

"Not at all, you two have a good time," Mrs. Bowden said, remembering she had met Jenna at Mass a few weeks back. "You're the girl I sat next to in church."

"Yes. I always sit in front when Jack is playing."

Pulling Jenna away from his mom by the hand, Jack yelled back, "Hey Mom, the study group downstairs is hungry."

Jack knew this decision to take Jenna into his room was quite the opposite of Wendy's wishes. However, at this moment he was weighing his future with Wendy. Did he really love her or was he with her because that was what Wendy wanted. He certainly was looking forward to Homecoming with Wendy, but he mostly feared her wrath. On the other hand, Jenna made him glow from within. His desire for Jenna's attention was now overwhelming and he just couldn't resist the temptation to spend more time with her.

Opening the door, Jack showed Jenna his room by sweeping his arm from one side to the other and proclaiming, "This is my room."

Jenna experienced sensory overload. The room was filled with posters, furniture, and trophies. Both Jack and Sam shared the same bedroom and between them both they had collected a large number of awards. Certificates of achievement hung from the walls and trophies occupied every available surface space.

Jack offered Jenna the desk chair but she opted to climb up to the top bunk. Swinging her legs, she commented on the décor, "Nice room. Which trophy is your favorite?"

Jack reached over to the corner of his desk and grabbed an enormous football trophy. "I guess this one. It's my most valuable player trophy from last year. My teammates gave it to me."

"It must be nice to have everyone think so highly of you," Jenna exclaimed, wishing she were as popular.

Jack paused for a second. He thought about what people really did think of him. He knew people depended on him quite a bit. Sometimes he wished he could just blend in like everyone else. But right now, the only person's opinion that mattered sat right in front of him.

"I suppose it's nice to have people in your corner," Jack confided. "But right now, I'm having a problem with Chuck Cruise. He's been picking on Sam."

"Everyone has a problem with Chuck," Jenna consoled.

Pausing, Jenna tried to change the subject. "You know what? I think you should play a song at the homecoming dance after the game."

"Oh yeah, you're the only one," Jack jested.

"Can you play me a song now?"

"Sure, what do you like?"

"Rock."

Pleasantly surprised, Jack smiled and asked, "Do you know this one?"

Jumping up, Jack began to play Kiss' "Rock and Roll All Night". Jenna kicked her feet from the top bunk in time with the music. When Jack reached the chorus, they both sang so loudly that the study group in the basement could hear it coming through the ceiling.

Jenna leapt off the bunk and danced while she sang. She then moved behind Jack and rubbed her back up and down his as she danced to the music. When Jack played the final chorus, everyone in the whole house, including his parents, were singing the lyrics. When the song ended, the study group applauded so that Jenna and Jack would know they had an audience.

"You're incredible," Jenna praised as she moved around to face Jack.

"You're too kind," Jack answered appreciatively.

Looking at her watch, Jenna gasped at the time and asked, "Can we watch Sports Central on TV?"

Paralyzed, Jack didn't know if heard Jenna correctly.

"Excuse me?" Jack blurted out.

"I need to watch Sports Central so I can see the today's college football highlights."

Jack had a difficult time believing that a beautiful teenage girl would ever watch Sports Central. Combine that with her love of rock music and Jenna seemed to be more like a guy than a girl.

"Sure," Jack said, now thinking that her interest in the show was just to impress him which made him like her even more.

When they entered the living room, Jack's parents were watching the weather channel so Jack didn't feel as if they would mind watching something else.

"Do you two mind if we watch Sports Central?"

Jack's father perked up and switched the channel while saying, "Mind? It would be my pleasure."

A commercial provided Jenna an opportunity to offer some insight into the national poll to Jack and his father. "Miami lost this week and Nebraska State beat Texas, so Nebraska State will definitely move into the top three. When Florida plays Florida State, they'll move into the top two if they can keep winning."

"Jenna's dad played for Nebraska State," Jack explained to his father.

"What position did he play?" Mr. Bowden inquired.

"Tight end," Jenna responded. "He didn't play that much but he still loves the program."

"Your dad is with the police department, isn't he?" Mr. Bowden asked to get some background.

"Yes. He was just promoted to Chief of Police last month."

Mr. Bowden was impressed, "Good to know."

"Hey, how do you get one of the little stars to put on your license plates so you can speed and not get pulled over?" Jack asked thinking of Wendy's driving habits.

Jenna responded with her hand out, "Give me fifty bucks and I'll see what I can do."

The show came back on and they sat, glued to the set. Jack's father, however, was more interested in Jenna's enthusiasm for football. He had no daughters of his own, so he was delighted at the prospect of a daughter-in-law that could love football the way he and his sons did. He watched her body move on the sofa with the players on the screen. It was as if she were carrying the ball and avoiding the tacklers. His eyes began to well up with tears of joy.

Jack turned to him to see his reaction to the highlights and saw tears rolling out of his eyes.

"You okay, Dad?" Jack asked with deep concern, drawing the attention of Jenna and Mrs. Bowden.

"Yeah, I'm fine," Mr. Bowden assured them, wiping away the moisture.

"What's up with the tears?" Jack said, getting embarrassed.

"I just got some dust in my eye," Mr. Bowden sniveled, trying to cover up the truth.

*

In a jovial mood, the team sat around the locker room. The sweat poured off the brows of the players while dirt and grass stained their uniforms. The noise of helmets rattling and cleats tapping the floor slowly came to a halt. It was halftime and the Screaming Eagles led Toll Gate 20-0.

Again, the Sacred Heart defense had done their homework and studiously memorized the plays and formations of the Toll Gate Titans. The defense had controlled the line of scrimmage and forced two Toll Gate fumbles deep in their own territory. Cruise and Singleton had scored touchdowns on short drives and the Screaming Eagles returned a punt for a touchdown right before the end of the half.

The players were relaxed and remained calm. Sacred Heart was headed for its third straight victory and hadn't given up a single point all season. Earlier in the season, the players were excited about winning by a large margin, but now they expected it. Domination was now the standard and anything less was unacceptable.

Coach Dawson spoke firmly, "I know it seems that we're invincible, but this game is far from over. We have to put them away. Do not relax. Keep hustling. Keep hitting."

The second half began and neither offense could generate a drive. The third quarter passed with an exchange of punts and no gains had been made in field position.

At the beginning of the fourth quarter, Sacred Heart took possession on its own twenty-five yard line.

Cruise called a pass play on first down, "X out on two."

Tanner lined up in the slot. On the signal, he ran up the field and faked in and cut out. Cruise, who normally threw the ball with great accuracy, threw the ball behind the receiver, right into the hands of the closest defender. With no offensive players in the flat, the Toll Gate defender jogged effortlessly in for a touchdown.

Trying to protect the lead, Coach Dawson called for a series of running plays to run down the clock. Starting on their own thirty-three, Singleton carried up the middle for two yards.

Then Cruise ran a quarterback option for three more on second down. On third and five, Dawson called for a pass to get the first down.

Cruise dropped back to pass and threw over the middle, but wide, and directly into the hands of the linebacker. The burly defender ran past Cruise on his way for another Titan touchdown. The Sacred Heart lead was down to six with four minutes left in the game.

"Damn it!" Coach Dawson swore at Cruise when he reached the sideline. "For crying out loud, you've got to tackle that guy."

Again, Sacred Heart received the kickoff and went back on offense and again, Coach Dawson called for running plays. On first and second downs, Singleton carried off tackle for gains of one and two yards. Thinking that he would rather put Jack and the defense back on the field rather than risk another interception, Dawson called for another run up the middle on third down. The play went only for one yard and Sacred Heart punted back to Toll Gate.

Only seventy-three yards separated Toll Gate from an unthinkable comeback but Jack and the defense were relentless in their attack. On first down, Ken sacked the quarterback for a loss of five. On second down, Jack broke up a screen and the pass fell incomplete. On third and fifteen, Toll Gate attempted a reverse. The Sacred Heart defense moved through the Titan line like water through a sieve and foiled the play. On fourth down, Toll Gate threw a Hail Mary that landed out of bounds. Sacred Heart took possession and the victory was theirs.

Cruise and his friends were laughing and joking as they walked from the field.

"3-0. We're on our way," Hamilton boasted about their win-loss record.

"The championship awaits," Singleton concurred.

"We got away with one tonight," Hamilton added, referring to the slim margin of victory.

"It was in the bag the whole time," Cruise laughed.

"What do you mean? You threw two INTs for touchdowns in the fourth quarter. If the defense hadn't stopped 'em, we would have lost," Hamilton interjected.

"Defense, schmefence, all I ever hear about is our defense. I'm telling you guys, it was in the bag," Cruise insisted.

It was apparent to Singleton that something was up. Cruise was practically taking credit for the interceptions. He couldn't understand how giving away points was helping the team. He didn't really want to know more than he already did. Singleton decided it was best to keep his mouth shut rather than fight with his closest friend.

Hamilton, however, was too stupid to realize what Cruise was saying. He broke the awkward silence with shouts of elation. "Another victory...means another victory party!"

Chapter 8

Mr. Bowden retrieved the Saturday Journal and was sitting down to breakfast. When he unwrapped the paper and pulled out the sports section, he discovered his son's picture on the front page. The problem was that picture was not of Jack, but of Sam. The picture was an 8 x 10 of Sam holding a red card extended in his right hand and the headline read, "Sacred Heart Turns Back Late Toll Gate Rally" and in somewhat smaller type, a related line read "Are the Screaming Eagles Playing Fair?"

Before reading the story, Mr. Bowden read the caption under Sam's picture. It read "Sam Bowden, third string quarterback, sends signals to the Screaming Eagles' defense. The defense leads the league in every statistical category and has not been scored upon yet this season." With nervous hesitation, Mr. Bowden went to the story and read. After making his way through the facts of the game, the story speculated on Sacred Heart's defensive success.

The story read:

A reliable source claims that the Screaming Eagles' defense knows each play that is being run before the ball is snapped. The source says that foul play is at hand and claims that the third string quarterback, Sam Bowden, has illegally obtained the plays and formations of its opponents. He signals the offensive play to his defense immediately prior to each play. The source speculates that Bowden has either stolen playbooks or is paying former players for information, or both.

Given the success of the Screaming Eagles' defense and the nature of the reaction of the players on the field to Sam Bowden's signals, an investigation has been undertaken by the State Athletic Association.

Overtaken by shock and dismay, Mr. Bowden called for his sons. "Jack, Sam, I think you had better take a look at this."

"What is it, Dad?" Jack yelled from his room.

"Just get in here, will you?"

Jack and Sam walked down the hall to the kitchen. Both were already a little afraid. They had heard that tone of their father's voice before and both suspected they were in trouble for something.

"Look at this," their father said, pointing to the paper.

"Oh my God!" Jack said when he saw the picture and headlines.

Both boys proceeded to read the story before offering further reaction. Jack began to feel light headed as he read. He knew this couldn't have a good ending. He had worked so hard to earn his reputation and the whole season could be down the toilet if the investigation found they were doing something wrong.

Once finished, Sam ended the silence. "I wonder if we were doing anything illegal."

"Why would you think that?" Mr. Bowden asked.

"I just assumed what we're doing was within the rules. I never researched it," Sam confessed, feeling guilty.

"Did you tell the coach?" Mr. Bowden probed.

"Sure, we told him. Remember at halftime of the Pilgrim game?" Sam said, knowing this wasn't exactly the truth.

Jack knew this wasn't even close to the truth. They hadn't told him anything. First, they lied to the coach and now they were lying to their father.

"Then it's his responsibility. I'm sure he's aware of the rules regarding this type of thing. You can't be faulted for hard work. That would just be wrong." Mr. Bowden stated as a matter of fact.

"Who would say that we stole playbooks or paid people for information?" Sam asked.

"It was probably the paper making the accusations. You know...to give the story more juice. So people will think it's real," Mr. Bowden guessed.

"Do you think it was that obvious? I mean we weren't showing signals to the crowd and it would be hard to see from the other side of the field," Sam thought aloud.

"I don't know who it was," Jack answered, "but I bet Coach Dawson has fire shooting out of ears right now."

Not fifteen minutes had passed and the phone rang. Mrs. Bowden answered the phone. She talked briefly before she covered the mouthpiece and said, "Sam, it's for you. It's Sports Central. They want to know if you would be willing to do an interview regarding the story in the paper."

Sam looked at Jack for approval.

"I don't think that's a good idea," Jack said. "You had better talk to the coach first."

"Oh, come on, it's Sports Central," Sam begged. "How often do you think I'll get to be on TV? If we talk to the coach, he won't let me. You know that. Besides, if we do this now, no one can say otherwise. Our reputation is at stake. We worked so hard and now they're saying we're cheating."

Mr. Bowden offered no opinion. Both boys seemed right and he just shrugged his shoulders, abstaining from the debate.

Sam took the phone and agreed to do the interview.

"You think Coach Dawson has fire shooting out of ears now, wait until Monday," Sam declared.

*

Matt, Kelly, and Wendy pulled into the Bowden's driveway. Matt had never been to Jack's house before and grimaced when he first saw it. Jack's house was a small ranch that had little character. Although it was freshly painted and its gardens were full of flowers, the house showed its age. The windows were odd shapes and the garage doors suffered from wear.

The springs brought the storm door back to its resting position with a loud thwack as Jack jogged out to Matt's car. Matt and Jack made eye contact right before Jack entered the back door of Matt's brand new Lexus. The plush seating and new car smell was foreign to Jack and he noticed it right away. He rubbed his hands on the seats, wishing that he were able to afford such luxury.

While Jack longed for material possessions, he was also aware that he was richer than most kids in many other ways. He thought about how his parents were still together after twenty-two years while most of his peer's folks had split up. He recalled stories his friends told of how their parents fought over money and kids. His family had no such disagreements and coming home was always a joyful event even if it were only from school.

Even though Jack was at peace with himself and his life, he still found himself envious of Matt when it came to his car. Jack guessed Matt's car had to cost more money than his family's three vehicles put together.

"This is a nice ride," Jack complimented, trying to get off on the right foot.

"Thanks," Matt said, turning up the radio so he wouldn't have to talk to Jack.

Jack gave Wendy an aggravated look. Wendy had convinced him to go on a double date, arguing that it might be nice to get to know Matt. She had said what a great guy he was and it was Jack that needed to "get over it".

"So…how was your day?" Wendy asked Jack.

"Did you see the paper?" Jack asked in response.

"I did," Matt piped in. Matt turned the radio down so he could expand the conversation. "Chuck told me what you guys were up to. I didn't think there was anything wrong with the signals. But I never thought you guys would stoop so low as to steal plays."

"Is that what Chuck told you?" Jack asked. "Did he imply we stole something?"

"He's just pissed because we're winning so easily. He never gets a chance to be the hero. He'll never lead a fourth quarter comeback with the way the defense is playing," Matt volunteered.

Jack began to put two and two together and wondered if Cruise was involved with the newspaper article. Surely, Cruise wouldn't risk the team's future for his personal gain. Thinking about how enraged Cruise had been on the sideline of the

Pilgrim game, Jack figured it must have been Cruise who was the source of the article. No one else was as big an ass as Chuck Cruise.

"Was Chuck the paper's source?" Jack asked point blank.

"You'll have to ask him. I don't know anything about that," Matt said, turning the radio up in order to end their dialogue.

"Hey, where are we going, anyway?" Jack asked Wendy.

"Dinner and a movie," Wendy whispered into his ear as she snuggled up to him in the spacious back seat.

Wendy's hot breath touched Jack and his anger vanished. Wendy ran her hand up his thigh and he instinctively moved his lips to meet hers. Their kissing intensified and they practically forgot there was another couple in the front seat.

"Guys!" Kelly shouted, trying to break them up. "No PDA!"

Smiling with no sign of embarrassment, Wendy reapplied her lipstick while Jack reclined in his seat.

"Where are we eating? I'm starved. I could eat an entire cow!" Jack boasted of his ability to eat large amounts of food.

"You could not eat a whole cow," Kelly mocked at the absurdity.

"I could eat more in one sitting than you could eat in four days," Jack calculated looking at her petite figure.

"No you couldn't. Besides, gluttony is not something I find appealing," Kelly said, losing her appetite.

Matt twisted himself in his seat and said to Jack, "I bet I can eat more than you."

"How much?" Jack asked in response to the impending challenge.

"Ten bucks."

"You're on."

Wendy looked at Kelly with disgust. "You two are not going to ruin our evening with some macho contest of seeing who can eat the most."

"Choose the place," Matt told Jack.

Jack set the conditions, "Pizza Palace. We order one pizza at a time and we each eat half. We keep eating until someone gives up...or pukes."

Matt made an abrupt left turn and both girls realized that their plans for a romantic dinner had ended. They would've refused to enter the restaurant if they hadn't been so hungry.

Wendy punched Jack in the arm and said, "Thanks a lot. You just ruined my evening."

"Oh c'mon. It's a bet," Jack said, seeking approval. "Let's have some fun. You can be my cheerleader."

Wendy frowned as she walked through the door.

*

Jack and Matt sat at opposite sides of the table assessing each other's determination. Matt was not as tall as Jack but he weighed about the same. He had a big mouth with big lips that took up a lot of room on his big face. He certainly looked as if he ate a lot. Jack, however, was full of confidence because he'd always eaten more than anyone else. He remembered the time he ate twelve hot dogs at a picnic last July and he left still hungry. Plus, Jack hadn't eaten all day and he was starving.

The boys ignored the girls when the waitress came to take their order. They took turns informing the waitress of their dining needs.

"We'll have a large cheese pizza every twenty minutes," Matt instructed.

"And we'll need a pitcher of water," Jack added, informing her of the contest. "We have a bet of who can eat the most pizza."

"How many pizzas do you think you can eat?" the waitress asked curiously.

Jack thought for a second and guessed, "I can eat four pizzas by myself."

"I can eat five," Matt countered with his nose in the air.

Kelly reacted with disgust, "If you eat five pizzas, I'm going to barf."

"We'll each have a salad and a diet cola," Wendy said, ordering for Kelly and herself.

Right before the waitress left, she said, "I'll talk to the manager to see if I can get you a group discount."

Before the first pizza showed up, the manager came over to talk to the group. "You boys play football for the Screaming Eagles?" he asked, looking at their letter jackets.

"Yeah, you go to the games?" Jack asked, trying to be polite.

"No, but according to the paper, you guys are having a heck of a year," he said enthusiastically. "I hear you boys are having a little contest. I'll tell you what, I'll treat you to all the free pizza you can eat, but I get to use the contest for publicity."

When the boys agreed, the manager had their table moved to the center of the restaurant and put a big blackboard behind them that read, "The Great Pizza Eating Contest: Jack Bowden vs. Matt Singleton." Then under the title, each boy had a column that read, "Number of Pizza's eaten."

The manager changed the size from large to small so he could make the numbers more impressive on the big blackboard.

The first pizzas arrived shortly thereafter and the boys dug in. The small pizzas were about a third of the large ones and went down quickly. The boys ate slice after slice. The first pizza was gone in less than five minutes. The second and third pizzas were consumed with equal speed. As the numbers of pizzas eaten were recorded on the blackboard, more and more customers became aware of the competition.

When each boy received their fourth pizza, people left their seats to come over to watch the boys chew and swallow. Some boys that had recently entered the restaurant knew Matt and stood behind him as if in his corner of a boxing match. They chanted his name in a low tone as he ate the last piece of the fourth pizza and then cheered wildly upon its disappearance.

Kelly and Wendy became annoyed at all of the attention their dates were attracting.

"I'm getting claustrophobic!" Wendy called to Kelly over all of the commotion.

"Let's move," Kelly suggested.

The girls left abruptly, unnoticed by Matt and Jack as each was receiving his fifth pizza.

With the crowd of onlookers growing, Jack showed off by folding a piece in half and shoving the entire slice in his mouth, much like a snake dislocating its jaw to swallow its meal whole. He had to look up to the ceiling to prevent the pizza from falling out of his mouth while he chewed. The crowd clapped in appreciation for the variant style of mastication. In an attempt to not be outdone, Matt held a piece level with his face and bit off piece after piece as fast as he could manage. His style of speed eating was met with equal applause.

When the manager recorded the fifth tally for each boy, the local newspaper reporter arrived to take pictures and interview the boys. The flash of the camera drew the attention of the entire restaurant and everyone left their seats to witness the carnage. The boys answered the reporter's questions with zeal and enthusiasm. When the reporter referenced the world record for eating, both boys became excited about the recognition they were receiving.

The marathon meal continued until the boys began their ninth pizza. The bites became smaller and taken less frequently. Jack could feel his stomach stretch to its capacity and he felt nauseous. He dreaded taking another bite, but Matt looked to be in the same condition. He could see Matt had reached his limit as well. He no longer was holding a slice in his hand and his head was facing the floor beneath the table.

Jack was sure that if he finished two more slices, he would win the contest so he bore on. He reached down into his competitive soul and began to build momentum. Bite after bite, he gained ground on Matt. Finally, he was down to one slice left. He used his hands to move his jaws up and down. He massaged his cheekbones as he chewed. He swallowed bravely anticipating victory with every passing minute. Matt's lack of progress only encouraged him more. With the last bit of crust gone, Jack raised his hands in the air and opened his mouth for the crowd to verify the slice and been completely ingested.

The crowd cheered and Matt conceded.

"You win," Matt proclaimed over the noise, slapping a ten dollar bill on the table.

The crowd departed upon Matt's concession. Wendy and Kelly returned to the table knowing the eating match had concluded. When Jack rose to greet Wendy, she approached him cautiously still annoyed that their date had turned sour.

"Well, who won?" she asked with her hands on her hips not really concerned about the outcome.

"I did," Jack said triumphantly.

Wendy commended Jack after assessing his protruding abdomen, "Congratulations, fat boy."

Kelly sized up her man and sighed, "I can't believe I just spent two and a half hours at Pizza Palace. What a colossal waste of time. Let's get out of here."

The couples started moving toward the door and both boys began to moan painfully.

In the parking lot, Jack doubled over and ran to a line of shrubs. In the greenery, he began to vomit with the pressure of a fire hose. Time after time, his body lurched forward and his mouth came unhinged. With each convulsion, he let out a cry like a wounded animal. The girls and Matt were instinctively repulsed and dared not to look.

Matt felt the saliva begin to stream into his mouth and the noise Jack was making sparked his own need purge his gigantic supper. Matt dashed over to the hedge and puked alongside Jack.

Both boys bent over with their hands on their knees trying to catch their breath between barfing fits.

"I want my money back," Matt demanded before he tossed another pizza.

"Take it, you lucky bastard," Jack said, handing the bill back.

"Lucky...why am I lucky?" Matt asked with contempt.

"You're lucky we didn't make it to the car."

Chapter 9

"Be quiet! It's coming on," Sam told his family as they stirred about trying to get a good vantage point for the story.

The Sports Central intro came on the screen and the commentators introduced the program with their regular humorous banter. Highlights from college football preceded images of Sam sending signals into the defense during the Toll Gate game.

"Holy cow! Did you see me?" Sam asked his family with uncontrolled excitement. Subconsciously, he stood up while the promos were rolling. "How did they get footage of the game? Did you see how the camera was directly on me? Wow! This is bigger than I thought."

The program continued after the commercial break and the Bowdens watched with tremendous anticipation. The show kept showing the same promo repeatedly which began to irritate Sam.

"When are they going to show it?" Sam asked every minute, expecting no one to answer.

"Shut up, will you? They said it would be in forty minutes thirty minutes ago," Jack answered, trying to calm his brother down.

At last, the story began. "Now from Warwick, RI, here's a story of one high school football team that has developed an advantage over its opponents. The Sacred Heart Screaming Eagles are playing the best defense in the entire country. They have allowed only six first downs, no points, and have held their opponents to an average of thirty total yards a game over the first three games of the season."

"With this unprecedented defensive success, the Screaming Eagles are now under investigation for illegally obtaining information regarding opponent's offensive plays. Shown here is Sam Bowden, freshman third string quarterback, using flash cards to signal his team the opponent's play. This unusual conduct has spurred many to believe that the Screaming Eagles are gaining an unfair advantage. We traveled to Warwick to speak with the scheme developer, Sam Bowden. Sam showed us how the system works," the commentator announced.

"First, we take tape of the opponent's games and digitize it on the computer. We then categorize each play by formation and situation. We break down each player package and then can easily predict run or pass. We also know what direction the play is going, and who will end up with the ball," Sam explained.

The screen shifted back and forth from Sam talking in the local TV studio to a video clip of the Screaming Eagles' defense tackling Toll Gate ball carriers.

"How are the signals relayed?" the TV analyst quizzed.

Hesitating briefly, Sam described the signal system. First, we identify the play from a chart we create from video, then we use color cards to relay the play to the defensive captains. The captains take appropriate action to audible the defense, if there is time, or shift their own positions to enable them to pursue the play more effectively."

"How would you rate the success of the system?" the commentator followed up without passing judgment.

"We've had tremendous success. I think our defense was already one of the best in the state. My brother, Jack, was an All-American last year at middle linebacker. The system has only enhanced the defensive performance," Sam said, giving credit to the defense. "You have to understand, our system is not just in place on game day. Each defensive starter gets their own video each Saturday and spends the week studying our next opponent. It's not enough to know the play, but also to know the player across the line from you. You have to learn the player's strengths and weaknesses in order to be successful."

"What do you say to those who claim this system gives you an unfair advantage?"

"I say that being prepared should be rewarded. And so far it has. Everyone has access to game tapes. If we work a little harder and study a little more, we should have an advantage. Football shouldn't be just about who's bigger, stronger and faster, it should be about being smarter, too."

The camera cut back to the studio, "There you have it. The Screaming Eagles are setting new standards in the lengths people will go to ensure success. They've clearly worked hard to get where they are, but the real question remains to whether or not the High School Athletic Association will endorse their practice."

The Bowdens relaxed in their chairs, clearly satisfied with the piece. Just as Jack opened his mouth to discuss the story, the TV commentator cut him off.

"In a related story, we also came upon this tape while we were in Warwick. Apparently, two of the Screaming Eagles had a little competition of their own."

The video went to an amateur video of Jack and Mark eating pizza.

"Screaming Eagles star linebacker, Jack Bowden defeated tailback Mark Singleton in a pizza eating contest Saturday. As you can see on the tally board, Bowden ate nine pizzas to eight for Singleton. Highlights include a single slice eaten in one bite by Bowden and then, following the competition, the duo purged the meal."

The video went to Mark and Jack puking in the bushes, and then to Wendy and Kelly's reaction. The girls involuntarily spun out of view, screaming in disgust.

"It seems these boys bit off more than they could chew," the analyst joked.

The program went to commercial and the Bowden's turned the TV off.

"Well, that was some story," Mr. Bowden offered. "You'll never be able to live that one down."

Jack was like a deer caught in the headlights. Never had he felt so betrayed and humiliated. He had never been the punch line of a joke. While it should have been easy to laugh at himself, he felt small and juvenile.

"You just can't stand it," Sam barked. "You can't let me have the spotlight for once, just once. I only ask for one time. I'm actually on Sports Central and you have to go and ruin it for me. Do you think anyone at school will be talking about

106

me? No! No one will even remember the part about me. They'll only remember you and Singleton puking pizza."

Sam walked out in a huff, refusing to wait for Jack's rebuttal.

*

Sam was wrong.

The next day at school everyone was talking about the story. The whole defensive unit congratulated him on his success. Girls he had only dreamed of were smiling and waving at him in attempt to attract his attention as he passed them in the halls. Even his teachers made notice of the story.

Upon his arrival to algebra class, Mr. Stamps commented on the story. "I watched Sports Central last night. You were pretty good."

The hair on the back of Sam's neck stood on end. He was certainly happy to have his classmates' attention, but having the approval of someone as smart as Mr. Stamps really meant the world to Sam. True joy and euphoria overcame Sam as he walked to his seat. He could barely acknowledge the compliments from the students he passed.

Just as he was nearing his seat, he passed Cruise.

Cruise caught his eye and sneered, "Loser."

Infuriated, Sam's blood began to boil. Sam began to obsess about Cruise. Thoughts of hate and malcontent passed through his mind. He thought about how much he wanted to hurt Cruise, just the way Cruise had hurt him four weeks ago. Sam looked at his arm and moved it from side to side and up and down. The arm was pretty much healed but the memory of the pain remained. Chuck Cruise was the biggest jerk he'd ever met.

Mr. Stamps began instruction by giving a few last minute tips on taking this morning's test. He talked about the various equations necessary to complete the problems. Although Sam had studied the night before and considered himself fully prepared, he couldn't concentrate on Mr. Stamp's lecture because his mind was fixed on Cruise.

Within minutes, Mr. Stamps was passing out the tests. He counted the number of students in each row and then handed the tests to the first person in the front. The first student in each row took one and passed the stack backward. This procedure for handing out assignments and other notices was normal routine. Sitting directly in front of Sam, Cruise always abused him by dropping his on the floor, or throwing it at him. Sam had become frustrated and was determined to ask Mr. Stamps for a new seat.

Sam, who sat in the last seat in his row, once again had to retrieve his test from the floor. And as times before, there was an extra copy of the test. Normally, Sam would have raised his hand and returned the extra copy to Mr. Stamps, but this time, he devised a scheme to get even with Chuck Cruise.

Sam went right to work on his test. With speed and accuracy, he completed problem after problem. For his devilish plan to work, he needed to finish his own test in record time. He was working so fast he felt like he was a computer.

When Sam was done with his test, he placed the extra copy on top of his. In the name blank, he entered Chuck Cruise. On this bogus test, Sam again worked every problem, intentionally making errors along the way in order to arrive at completely wrong answers. He proceeded to fill out the test missing every single problem. When Sam reached the final problem, he began to laugh inside himself. He couldn't wait to see Cruise's expression when he got this test back.

Once done, Sam waited patiently for Cruise to finish his test. Sam knew this part of his plan was the most crucial. Cruise collected his belongings and got out of his seat. He placed his test on the stack on Mr. Stamp's desk right before he exited the room.

With Cruise out of the room, Sam stood. He placed his own test on top of the bogus test and walked up to the front of the room. Luckily, Mr. Stamps became distracted when another student asked for some clarification. Sam put the two tests on the stack and removed Cruise's original test. He jammed Cruise's test into his coat pocket and left the room.

When Sam looked down the hall, he saw Coach Dawson against the bright sunlight glaring through the window. Coach Dawson's silhouette grew larger as the coach approached him. Sam's throat began to swell with anxiety. He reached inside his coat pocket and felt Cruise's crumpled test. Immediately, Sam's mind began to churn. He thought of all the possible consequences if he were caught with Cruise's test. He wondered if this mischievous act could be considered criminal, or if expulsion was the worst possible outcome.

As Coach Dawson got closer, Sam put on a pseudo smile and offered a forced greeting. "Hi, Coach."

"Sam, we need to talk football."

Sam relaxed a little and asked, "Yeah, what's up?"

"I just got off the phone with the Athletic Association. They saw the story on TV last night." The coach paused for affect while he adjusted his ball cap. "They weren't all that happy about our defensive tactics. They recognized that, technically, we are operating within the rules, but they feel the system violates the spirit of the game. They are asking us to stop using the signals from the sidelines and we're going to comply."

"But Coach, the defense has worked really hard."

"Hold on Sam, I'm not finished. They didn't say we couldn't use film. We're still going to use it, but we're going to take it a step further. You, my little friend, are going to start at free safety on the defense."

"You mean . . . play defense?"

"Yup. You already know it. You can call the audibles and since you'll be the free safety, you won't have any responsibility other than to attack the ball."

"But Coach, I don't think I'm ready." Sam protested, thinking about how big the seniors were and how hard they hit.

"You'll do fine," Coach Dawson said, assessing Sam's size. "You might, however, consider visiting the weight room between classes."

Sam had no response and the two stood in the corridor staring at each other.

Coach Dawson broke the awkward silence, "Well, see you at practice."

Again, Sam said nothing and Coach Dawson felt compelled to say something as he walked away. "By the way, you looked good on TV. Jack...not so much."

*

The cafeteria hummed with chatter. Making his way through the line, Sam paid for his meal and went to sit down. Passing through the dining room, he could feel eyes upon him. Every now and again a student would say hi or wave. Sam could see his normal lunchroom companions and honed in on their location. When he closed in on their table, Ken greeted him.

"Hey pal, how's it going? Here, sit next to me, I'm having some trouble with my history. I was wondering if you could help me make sense of it."

Sam enjoyed his resident status as an expert in all areas of academia. He was happy to sit where he was needed.

He couldn't control himself and pulled Cruise's test out of his coat and showed it to Tim.

"What's that?" Tim inquired before recognizing it as the test he just took.

"It's Chuck's test. I got an extra one at the end of the row and I filled out a phony with all wrong answers," Sam said, breaking into a laughing fit that made him double over.

"Holy Jesus, are you drunk?" Tim gasped.

Mark reached across the table and ripped it from Tim's hands. He quickly scanned the paper and remarked, "You're going to get in so much trouble."

"So, he's been picking on me all year. I think it's worth it."

"I'd burn this right now," Mark whispered, handing it back to Sam.

"I can't wait to see his expression when he gets his test back. He's going to freak," Sam stuttered, bursting into laughter once again.

"How'd you do, Ken?" Tim asked, referring to the very same test.

"Okay, I guess. Our study group has been paying big dividends. I couldn't even do single variable equations before this year."

While the other boys discussed the various problems on the test, Sam reviewed Cruise's test. He went through each line and soon discovered that Chuck had missed every single problem and it became obvious that Cruise would have failed the test anyway.

"Oh my God! Look at this," Sam shouted. "He missed all of them."

"What?" Tim asked.

"Look," Sam said, pointing to Cruise's paper. "He missed every problem. He didn't get anything right. What a moron!"

*

The next day in math class, Mr. Stamps held the tests in his hand as he prepared to return them to the class.

"I am going to give back the tests now. Before I do, I want to recognize a few people for their outstanding work, Mark 95, Victoria 93, Sarah 96, Tim 90, Ken 97 and Sam 100."

Mark, Tim, and Ken showed no humility, got up out of their seats, and began bowing like actors at the end of a play. Some smattering of applause followed to honor those students. Sam was not surprised by his own achievement but was elated that his friends had done so well.

Mr. Stamps walked down the rows passing back the tests. When he handed Cruise his test, Sam's study group strained to get a view of the grade. Sam looked at Chuck's grade and it said 71. Sam couldn't believe his eyes. He knew Mr. Stamps awarded partial credit for showing work, but a 71 seemed extremely generous for not answering a single question right. Then remembering what Cruise's original test was like, Sam understood how much better his version was than Chuck's.

Mr. Stamps even complimented Cruise as he passed by. "Nice work, Chuck. It's good to see you improving."

Cruise even gave a high five to Hamilton before stuffing the test in his bag.

Sam shook his head in disbelief, while the others giggled to themselves.

*

Friday rolled around and the Screaming Eagles traveled to Cranston West to face the Falcons. Cranston West was a notoriously weak team and Sacred Heart pummeled them on a regular basis. The previous year, Sacred Heart won 38-0 and the players expected another rout.

The crowd was unusually large because of the Screaming Eagles recent publicity. Not only was the student body jumping on the bandwagon, but high school football fans from all around the state wanted to see their highly touted defense. Fans poured into the stadium under the cold September sky.

The fans clapped with vigor every time the Screaming Eagles' defense took the field and roared with approval when the defense created a turnover or stopped a drive. The defense fed off of the energy of the crowd and the hitting intensified with each passing quarter.

Sam started at free safety, just as Coach Dawson had said. He had no trouble learning his assignments after a full week of practice. The defense listened intently for Sam to call the plays. He identified the backs and the formations. He recognized the positioning of linemen and the motion of receivers. He called each play as if he were in the offensive huddle. Play after play, the defense surged through the offensive line to tackle the Falcon runners for losses. When they dropped back to pass, Sam overloaded the linemen with blitzing linebackers, and double covered the Falcons' intended receivers.

The defense dominated like never before. The Falcons gained no first downs and netted a loss of twenty-six yards. Sam intercepted two passes and returned one for a touchdown. The Screaming Eagles won the game 52-0.

Following the game, Coach Dawson attempted to bring the players together amidst a mini celebration in the locker room.

"Hey, hey, quiet down! Quiet down!" Coach Dawson yelled, trying to get his players attention without ruining the festive atmosphere.

Players continued to misbehave in a playful manner. As they stripped their uniforms off, tape and t-shirts flew through the air across the locker room. The noise actually got louder as more players became involved in the ruckus.

"Quiet please . . . Quiet please . . . SHUT THE HELL UP!" Coach Dawson boomed at the top of his voice.

The team stopped in their tracks.

Jack and his buddies had just returned with Sam from the shower room where they were giving him his congratulatory drenching after his first game on defense. They dropped Sam on the floor and stood at attention. Having just been dragged into the showers still in uniform, Sam slowly made it to his feet while the team waited for Coach Dawson to continue. With Coach Dawson staring directly at him, Sam's smile faded and he stood in a pool of water that had formed around his feet.

"I'd like to thank you all for a game well played. We kicked the snot out of them tonight!" Coach Dawson remarked with a huge grin.

The team gave a controlled cheer.

"Game ball," Coach Dawson shouted, holding the ball over his head, "goes to Sam Bowden."

The team cheered louder this time. The defense then hoisted Sam up in the air and hauled him back to the showers for another soaking.

Chapter 10

It was one thirty in the morning and Sam still couldn't sleep. He stared at the ceiling through the darkness of the night replaying the game in his mind. He envisioned the game in slow motion. He saw himself running between a Cranston receiver and the ball. He could see his hands outstretched before him and ball slide half way through his grasp before he clamped down on it. He recalled the crowd cheering wildly as he headed toward the end zone. He remembered how he faked the quarterback with a shoulder to the left before heading right. He recalled stiff arming a would-be tackler to the ground before heading to pay dirt. Sam's body flinched in his bed as he braced his body prior to his teammates tackling him in the end zone. The crushing pressure of his friends lying on top of him was accompanied by their jovial cries of happiness.

Sam rolled over onto his side still clutching the ball Coach Dawson had awarded him. He looked around his room at all of the trophies that surrounded him. They couldn't compare to the prize he now held. He rubbed his hand over the pigskin and placed his fingers between the laces in a slow methodic manner.

He gripped the ball loosely, rolled again on his back, and gently tossed the ball upward. He caught it just like he did earlier during the game. This football was his greatest treasure and last night's game was his greatest achievement.

At that moment, Jack opened the door and silently disrobed, trying not to disturb his brother. Jack didn't realize that Sam was awake and slipped into bed as quietly as possible. All along, Sam watched his brother and hoped he would start a conversation about the game. Sam loved his brother and often sought out his approval. He enjoyed nothing more than to have his brother praise his accomplishments.

After waiting thirty seconds, Sam couldn't hold out any longer and opened the dialog. "Good night, Jack."

"Good night," Jack repeated clinching his teeth, wishing he were already asleep.

"Where'd you go after the game?' Sam quizzed.

"Party," Jack responded with the least number of words possible, trying to show lack of enthusiasm.

"Who was there?" Sam asked, delaying his analysis of last night's game.

"The usual.Ken, Tim, Wendy, Mark, and Jenna."

"Jenna?"

"Yeah, Jenna."

"I like Jenna," Sam remarked. "She's so much nicer than Wendy. I wish you would go out with her instead."

"Shut up. I don't want to hear this," Jack said as he rolled over.

"I don't know what you see in Wendy. She's so mean and you know how Mom feels about her."

"Good night," Jack said, attempting to terminate the conversation.

"I think Jenna is the one for you," Sam remarked.

"If you say one more word, I'm going to make you sleep under my bed tonight."

Thinking back, Jack didn't make threats. He made promises. Sam remembered how Jack had said that once before and how he ended up under Jack's bed. He remembered yelling for his mom and dad to free him. That didn't help because after Jack pounded him, he was the one that got into trouble for waking up his parents. He didn't want to ruin his perfect evening by waking up the whole house.

But I want to talk about how great I did tonight, thought Sam. I want you to say what a fantastic football game it was and how tremendous I played. Sam opened his mouth and then closed it. This conversation could wait until morning.

*

The good times continued to roll. The Screaming Eagles won their next three games. They beat Mt. Hope 30-0, Cranston East 37-7 and North Kingstown 65-13. They were 7-0 and had already qualified for the playoffs. Jack and Sam continued to dominate the sports pages and with the team drawing college scouts, even Chuck was playing his best.

The team had just finished practice and the players were walking into the locker room ready to shower and disperse.

Jack's voice filled the locker room. "Everyone take a seat. We have some business." Pausing for the shuffling to subside, he looked about the room for attention. "As captain, it is my duty to conduct nominations for homecoming queen. Every year, the football team nominates the candidates and the student body elects the queen. The nominees must be seniors and this year, they must all be females. I open the floor for nominations."

The underclassmen knew not to speak. They knew they were there for formality only. Everyone understood that the seniors were in charge of this process.

Tim raised his hand and Jack called upon him. "I nominate Wendy Thompson."

Everyone knew Tim was nominating Wendy as a courtesy to Jack because the team knew how awkward it would be for Jack to nominate his own girlfriend.

Jack smiled at the gesture and seconded the nomination to the chuckling of the team.

Once the laughter ceased, Chuck raised his hand, cleared his throat and said, "I nominate Kelly Singer."

Hamilton seconded the motion before Jack could ask for one.

Jack knew Wendy would be thrilled that her best friend was also a nominee. Now, all he had to do was get Wendy's other close friend, Sue Rich, to be the third nominee and he would reap huge dividends in the romance department with Wendy.

Silence fell upon the room while the players contemplated the third nomination. Jack waited for a full minute before he spoke. "We need one more. Anyone? Does anyone have any ideas?"

Jack paused and just as he was about to nominate Sue, Sam raised his hand.

Shaking his head quickly from side to side, Jack was trying to get Sam to put his hand down, but Sam refused. Finally, Jack called upon his little brother.

"What? What is it Sam?"

"I would like to nominate Jenna Witherspoon."

Before Jack could object, Chuck dismissed Sam's nomination. "Nominations are for seniors, you idiot! When Jack said anyone, he didn't mean you."

The defensive players sneered at Cruise for his abrasiveness, but agreed in principle.

"Chuck is right, Sam. I was talking to the seniors. Does any senior have a nomination?" Jack clarified.

"Yeah, I do," Mark rang in. "I nominate Jenna Witherspoon."

"And I second that nomination," Tim yelled. Tim spun his body toward Chuck and added, "What do you think of those apples, Chuckle Head?"

Chuck lunged from his seat and dove at Tim. Tim anticipated Chuck's volatility and dodged his off balance body. Chuck hit his head on the steel grated locker and put a deep gash in his forehead. He rolled off the concrete bench and onto the floor. Blood gushed from Chuck's forehead and started pooling around his head."

"Damn! Look at all that blood," Tim commented, feeling a little responsible. Tim stood over him and apologized while several of the team members ran to get the coaches.

"I'm real sorry you got hurt," Tim said, feeling remorse.

The coaches pushed the gathering of players away from Chuck and wrapped his head with towels and tape. Coach Dawson called rescue and Chuck was put on a gurney. The team stood in silent shock as he was taken away.

*

"C'mon Tim, it wasn't your fault," Mark consoled. "He had it coming to him. It's not like anyone gives a damn about Chuck Cruise. He's the biggest butt head in school history."

Tim was so bummed, he barely heard what Mark was saying.

Jack eyed a burnt fry on his tray and internally debated eating it since it was the very last one. He thought about how Cruise's injury would affect the team. At last, he put the fry down and said what everyone else was already thinking. "Chuck is going to miss this week's game with East Providence. EP hasn't lost a game and we're going to need to score some points to win. We finally need the bastard, and he gets hurt in the locker room."

Tim, Mark, and Ken absorbed Jack's words and slumped in their seats. The Screaming Eagles' perfect season was in serious jeopardy. The boy's thoughts shifted to Buck Walters, Chuck's back up at quarterback.

"Buck's not going to be able to hack it. We don't have a chance," Mark declared.

"He can't play. He's just no good," Ken agreed.

Mark slammed his milk carton on the table and proclaimed, "Sam's got game experience. He's got confidence. He's real smart. He's just better, plain and simple. We have to find a way for Sam to play quarterback."

The boys brainstormed for the next five minutes on how to convince Coach Dawson that Sam would be a better choice. In the end, however, they agreed that if Sam were to be quarterback, he would have to prove himself in practice. They also agreed to show Walters no mercy in scrimmage, hoping they could make their point to Coach Dawson.

Just as the boys were finishing their lunch, Wendy walked toward their table.

"Oh, crap. I can tell by the look on her face she's pissed," Jack whispered to his buddies underneath the smile he was projecting in Wendy's direction.

The other boys sat motionless, giving their full attention to Wendy who stood at the head of the table.

"Okay, which one of you idiots nominated Jenna Witherspoon for homecoming queen?"

Wendy's eyes scoured each boy with the 'I'm going to kill you' look before coming to rest upon Jack.

None of the boys answered until Jack felt obligated to respond. "Don't look at me. I didn't do it."

"Weren't you in charge of the nominations?"

"Yeah, but I can't tell the players who they can nominate."

"Don't you realize that I really want to win homecoming queen?"

"I figured as much."

"Don't you realize how much I despise Jenna Witherspoon?"

"Yeah . . ."

"Didn't you know I was going to be angry?"

"Yeah, I knew this was going to happen."

"So, do you remember that little thing we had planned for homecoming night after the game?"

"Yeah . . ."

"It's off if I don't win homecoming queen! So you had better make sure I do. Got it?"

Wendy marched off without waiting for a reply.

Jack looked down at his plastic lunch tray for another morsel of food but found none. Then he looked up to find his three friends all staring at him.

"Well, that went well," Jack concluded. "Thanks a lot, you rejects."

Mark, Ken, and Tim responded in unison. Starting with hushed voices and gradually increasing their amplitude, they chanted, "Dump her! Dump her! Dump her!" Then as Tim noticed Jenna walking up to the group from behind Jack, he changed the chant to, "Jen-na! Jen-na! Jen-na!" The other boys followed and soon the volume was such that Jenna blushed in recognition.

Jack could see the boys' attention focused over his shoulder and guessed Jenna was now standing directly behind him. He slowly turned around and Jenna's smile beamed from her gorgeous face.

"Congratulations on your homecoming nomination. Your humble subjects await your royal proclamation," Jack said with a straight face, offering no hint of sarcasm.

"Thank you. Thank you all," Jenna responded, making a proper English curtsey. "May I sit with you?"

"Surely, you jest. We are mere peasants and you, my lady, are a princess. I am afraid that you must make friends with ladies Wendy and Kelly if we are to have any social interaction at all," Mark replied, continuing the façade.

"If that be the case then I renounce my nomination, for I have neither the strength nor the will to rule with the required degree of contempt and malice," Jenna began, deepening her pseudo English accent. Throwing her head to the side and raising the back of her hand to her forehead, she continued, "I, instead, throw myself at your mercy and beg your forgiveness. I have forsaken your gratitude and pissed off your girlfriend."

The boys broke free with laughter. Even Jack couldn't resist the humor of such a performance.

*

Chuck stood on the sideline in street clothes watching practice with a huge bandage wrapped around his head. Even though he didn't injure his eye, the wrap covered his left eye

122

making the injury appear much worse than it was. He stood with his arms folded assessing his replacement.

Both the offense and the defense simultaneously broke their huddles. Buck Walters followed the center to the line. He barked the signals and took the snap. He dropped back to pass and was sacked before he had an opportunity to look downfield. Two plays later, Walters was on the ground holding his wrist, moaning in pain.

The offense gathered around and watched as the coaches helped him to the sideline.

Coach Dawson motioned for Sam. Sam ran over to the coach before entering the huddle. "Okay kid, you ready?"

"Yeah," Sam mumbled through his mouthpiece.

"You know the plays?"

"Yeah."

"The signals?"

"Yeah."

"Let's see what you got," Coach Dawson said, looking up at the sky, hoping the football gods would smile down upon him.

Meanwhile, Jack and company were plotting in the huddle.

"Okay, Mark, you got what you wanted. Walters is out and Sam is in. Don't go soft now. We have to make him earn it. It's not going to be easy Friday against East Providence. Let's show him what it's really going to be like."

Sam called the play as instructed by Coach Dawson. "X curl, Z out, on two." Sam brought the offense to the line. Sam could see the defense was bearing down and knew they were coming after him. He looked straight into the eyes of his brother on the opposite side of center.

Calling the signals, he could see the safeties pinching the line, coming on a blitz. "Down, set, hut one, hut two."

The ball hit the heel of his hand and rebounded to the ground. He fell on it as four other players dove on top of him, forcing his elbow into his rib cage. Sam yelled for the players to get off, hoping the release of pressure would lessen the discomfort.

"C'mon, you wussy!" Hamilton taunted.

Sam held his tongue because he needed Hamilton to block for him.

After apologizing, Sam called the same play.

The defense blitzed again and Jack blasted Sam from behind, sending his frail body to the turf with great speed.

Sam was hurt, but not injured.

When he rolled over, Jack was standing above him with his hand outstretched to help him to his feet.

"So this is how it's going to be?" Sam queried as he checked his equipment for missing parts.

"Yeah, this is how it's going to be Friday, when East Providence comes a knocking," Jack replied as a matter of fact.

Sam collected himself and went back to the huddle. With no other quarterbacks available, Coach Dawson had no choice but to leave him in.

"Let's try counter sweep left on one," Sam said, needing a break from the pass rush.

When Sam walked his team up to the line, he could tell the defense recognized the formation almost instantly and shifted its linebackers and safeties to the left side. Sam knew the play was going for a loss before he called the signals.

Sam took the ball from center and as he turned to pitch the ball to Singleton, he decided to keep it and go the opposite way. The offense and defense moved to the left and Sam ran around the right end untouched and sprinted down the sideline.

Mark gave chase and sixty yards up the field, he pushed the young Bowden down out of bounds, two yards shy of a touchdown.

Sam tumbled to the ground and spun head over heels. Both Sam and Mark burst out laughing but couldn't be heard because they were so far down the field.

As they jogged back to the scrimmage line, Mark gave Sam his due, "Nice play, you did well." Mark went as far as to offer Sam some further success. "I'll give you some room on a post pattern."

Considering the offer, Sam responded, "No thanks. Bring your best, because I'm bringing mine."

"You got it."

Now, knowing Mark was likely to become aggressive, Sam called for an out and up. "Give me some time and I know I can hit it," Sam told his offensive line.

Singleton, becoming encouraged, said, "I'm staying in to block. Let's do this."

Sure enough, the blitz was on again and Singleton stepped up to hit Jack straight on. Tanner sold the route to Mark and Sam hooked him with a pump fake. Once the defenders bit on the out, Tanner turned it up, and Sam lofted a deep spiral that Tanner ran under. Tanner caught the pass in full stride with no defenders in sight.

"Touchdown!" Singleton called out as the two units watched Tanner stroll into the end zone. Singleton held his hand out in Sam's direction and said, "Give me five, dude!"

Sam slapped the hand and jogged back into the huddle as the offense pushed him around congratulating their joint success.

Sam and the offense enjoyed their best day against the defense in weeks. Sam's play could only be characterized as unbelievable. Everyone was impressed, even Chuck Cruise. Unfortunately for Sam, Cruise felt threatened and was determined to sabotage Sam's future at quarterback.

Chapter 11

Miraculously, Chuck recovered from his head injury and was ready to play the next day at practice. He performed like a collegiate All-American on the verge of a national championship. He hit everything he threw. He completed twelve of thirteen passes including four touchdowns. He led the team up and down the field like a man possessed.

Coach Dawson was delighted about his starting quarterback's return to action and totally dismissed the idea of Sam starting Friday's game. Although he was happy to have a competent back up, Coach Dawson gave no explanation to Sam regarding Chuck's reinstatement. All he said was, "Chuck's starting on Friday. You're number two."

When Jack and Mark heard the story from Sam, they were disappointed, but understood completely.

"Surely, you understand that playing against the Townies is far more intimidating than playing against your brother and his friends. Chuck's good. He's a jerk, but we aren't 7-0 because he's a lousy quarterback," Jack explained, trying to make his brother feel better. "C'mon, you're the only freshman varsity football player in the whole city. You can't be that upset. Anyway, where would we be if you were concentrating on offense?"

Sam hung his head in disappointment, but was encouraged to hear his brother speak so highly of him.

When Friday's game began, the Screaming Eagles dominated on both sides of the ball. The defense stopped the Townies twice in a row and the offense scored a touchdown on a thirty-two yard strike from Cruise to Tanner.

Then disaster struck for the Sacred Heart defense. Ken left the game with a bruised thigh and Matt Wilks, the Screaming Eagles' defensive end, broke an ankle. After the ambulance took Matt to the hospital, the defensive line was as porous as sandstone. The Townies oversized offensive line pushed the Screaming Eagles' replacements back like dominoes. Not even Jack and Mark, playing run all the way, could stop the onslaught.

First, it was three and four yards at a crack. Then as the second quarter wore on, East Providence was gaining eight to ten yards a play. The Townies scored three times in a row and led at the half, 21-14.

For the first time all year, the Screaming Eagles were in a dogfight and had their backs to the wall. Working like a madman, Coach Dawson scrawled on the blackboard. He showed his players the Townies' strengths and weaknesses. He devised a strategy of ball control offense and deep penetration on defense. He knew luck must be on his side to win this football game.

The tide shifted in the third quarter back to the Screaming Eagles. The Townies fumbled on their first possession and

Cruise capitalized on the mistake with an eighteen yard bootleg for the tying touchdown.

The Screaming Eagles' defense raised their intensity to a new level. While they gave up several first downs, they denied the Townies any scoring drives. Both teams traded punts.

It wasn't until late in the fourth quarter that the Screaming Eagles caught their big break. Sam recognized the Townie formation for a reverse and called a safety blitz audible for Mark. Mark raced toward the line of scrimmage as the quarterback took the ball. Instead of chasing the ball, Mark cut in front of the intended runner and intercepted the pitch. He outran a pack of Townies for the go ahead touchdown.

The celebration began when the Townies fumbled on the next series and Sacred Heart recovered on the East Providence twenty-eight. With only three minutes left in the game, it looked like a lock for Sacred Heart.

Then, with the game nearly in hand, on a pitchout to Singleton, Cruise didn't even come close. He pitched the ball so high and slow that the Townie safety easily intercepted the ball and ran the other way seventy-five yards for what appeared to be a tying touchdown. The Townies lined up for the extra point. Luckily for Sacred Heart, the kicker hit the upright and the ball bounced straight back. The Screaming Eagles won by a single point, 28-27.

When the players entered the locker room, they were emotionally drained. They had won the football game but didn't exactly feel good about how it happened.

"Wow, were we lucky or what?" Tim wondered aloud as he sat stunned next to his locker.

"Lucky is right. How would you like to be the East Providence kicker right now?" Mark added. "He's got to feel like a big turd. He'll be lucky if he ever plays again."

"Or to live," Cruise joked as he walked past.

"Hey, you had a nice game there Choke . . . I mean Chuck," Mark quipped in reference to his errant pitch that nearly cost them the game.

"What did you call me?" Cruise barked, seeking an apology.

"You heard me, Choke. Yeah, that's right Choker," Mark taunted. "If you want a piece of me, bring your sorry ass over here!"

Chuck dove for Mark. Mark moved and Chuck hit his head on the locker and rebounded to the floor. Chuck rolled over and blood was streaming from his head.

Tim walked over to Mark and both boys stood over Chuck staring down at his mangled face.

"Damn, déjà vu," Tim remarked.

"Yeah, but this time the cut is on the other side," Mark observed, pointing out how both cuts pointed to the middle of Chuck's head. I like it better this way. Symmetry is a good thing."

*

The red Firebird stopped abruptly next to a fire hydrant and when Jack shifted in reverse, the car rolled back to legal status. Sam got out of the car first and Jack followed. They strolled up the front walk of Tim's house together. Sam had never been to Tim's house before and guessed the house was four times the size of his own. The house cast a shadow so long, Sam estimated it was thirty feet high at the peak. They rang the bell and heard it echo inside the front hall. A few seconds later, Tim opened the door, expecting their arrival.

"Hi guys," Tim greeted, extending an arm inward.

"Hey Tim, how's it going?" Jack responded in a way Tim had heard a million times before.

Sam was overtaken by the vast marble entryway and didn't hear Tim's answer.

"Happy birthday, Sam. What are you now, fifteen?" Tim asked, pointing out his youthful age. "The party is out back."

Jack and Sam followed Tim to the backyard where the majority of the guests were already waiting. Jack saw that Tim had invited half of the team.

Jack knew that Wendy and her friends wouldn't be coming today. When Jack invited Wendy to Sam's birthday party two weeks ago, she quickly dismissed the idea and informed him that she would be in Boston that day. That was just fine with Jack because he knew everyone would be uncomfortable with her around. Jack relished the idea of being able to relax free from her demands.

"The burgers are ready," Mr. Watson called out from behind the grill. Wearing an apron and a chef's hat, Mr. Watson was doing the best he could. From Sam's perspective, the amount of smoke bellowing out of the grill made it seem like the whole thing was ablaze.

"Thanks, Dad," Tim replied, encouraging everyone to get some food while it was available. "Come and get it," Tim yelled. Lowering his voice he told Jack, "You can only have two burgers. You understand, right?"

Jumping from his seat, Jack got in line first to make sure he had an adequate amount of food to satisfy his growling stomach. With his food in hand, he made a place for himself and his buddies at a table next to the pool. Overlooking the water, Jack washed down his burger with a big swig of his soda.

Tim, Sam, Ken, and Mark all joined Jack. The boys were too hungry for conversation. Not a word was spoken until all the food had been consumed. The boys reclined in their chairs and proceeded to toast the previous evening's victory.

"How's the thigh?" Jack asked Ken, pointing to the heat pack Ken had attached to his pants.

"Hurts like hell, but I'll be back next week," Ken said while eating his second piece of pie. "Can't say as much for Wilks. He'll be at home for at least another week and he'll miss the rest of the season for sure."

Jack congratulated Mark again for his game winning touchdown. "That was some play. I've never seen anything like that. I bet you win a scholarship for that play alone."

Modest and giving, Mark accepted the compliment but passed on the credit. "Thanks, but it was Sam who made the call. He's the one who sniffed it out. It took me about three seconds to make the adjustment. I was lucky I moved in time."

Sam was elated that Mark was so generous. Sam didn't say a word. Mark had said enough. Sam felt honored to be amongst such terrific people. Yes, they were Jack's best friends but they were Sam's best friends, too.

"Hey, what's up with Choke?" Tim asked, continuing the banter.

The boys instantly understood the reference to Chuck and sprayed mouthfuls of soda in a fit of laughter. Ken started pounding his soda glass on the table as he choked on his pie. Tim heaved so violently that his chair tipped over and he spilled onto the grass. Jack was laughing so hard that his voice was silent and tears were rolling out of his eyes. Finally, the ruckus calmed down and the boys breathed huge sighs trying to get it out of their systems. Every time one of the boys tried to restart the conversation, the whole group started laughing again. Pretty soon all five of them fell, one by one, out of their chairs and onto the lawn with their bodies shaking with uncontrolled laughter.

Just as the joke lost its punch and the boys lifted themselves off the lawn, Jack saw Jenna and her girlfriends come around the corner of the house. The girls looked different than usual. Each wore jeans, a sweatshirt, and sneakers which was a tremendous departure from the normal skirt and heels. Their hair seemed different to Jack as well. Each girl in the group had it pulled back into a tight ponytail. Jenna, leading the girls through the party, cradled a football.

"Anyone for a game of football?" she shouted, making a grand entrance.

The boys were stunned and couldn't answer. They just stared in shock.

Jack turned to Tim and asked in a whisper, "Did you invite Jenna and her friends?"

"Yup," Tim burped.

Smiling, Jack declared, "You're the man!" Then he turned to face Jenna and asked, "Touch or tackle?"

"Only wussies play touch," Jenna answered with a challenge in her tone.

"Boys against the girls?" Jack asked, expecting a battle of the sexes.

"Of course," Jenna responded, pitching the ball to Jack. "You kick off."

Jack caught the ball and turned to rally his team. They put their drinks down on the table and jogged out to the center of the backyard. Jack's team spread out to make a line to cover the kick, but Jack called them into a huddle.

133

"We need some rules," Jack began. "Only tackle the girl that has the ball. Make sure she doesn't get hurt. Wrestle her to the ground."

"Then we all jump on her," Mark added.

"No! Don't piss 'em off. If we're really nice, maybe they'll stay awhile after the game," Jack reasoned. "No bra popping or butt grabbing...be gentlemen."

"So tell me again...why are we playing this game?" Tim asked.

"You heard me," Jack commanded, looking each boy in the eye to gain compliance.

When Jack had agreement, the boys broke the huddle and threw the ball down to the girls. Victoria caught the ball and dashed back up the field. The boys gave chase but the food slowed them down significantly. After crossing the goal line, Victoria threw the ball in the air and began whooping it up. After dancing and skipping in a circle, the other girls joined her for a touchdown dance.

Apparently, the girls had choreographed a routine for their touchdown celebration. They swung their hips in an eyebrow raising manner. Their bodies moved in sync from side to side, and then they finished with high fives all around. When they turned to go back up the field, the guys were standing motionless with mouths open, hoping the celebration would continue.

As the girls passed, Jenna said to Jack, "Do you like our moves?"

"Most definitely," Jack replied and added, "Without question."

The girls kicked to the boys. Sarah threw the ball to Sam. Sam caught the ball and ran as fast as he could but he didn't get any blocking and five girls tackled him at once. Sam lay at the bottom of a pile of female flesh.

Tim stood over the mound of bodies and remarked, "Sam, you are one lucky guy."

Sam got up and exclaimed, "Those girls hit harder than Cranston West."

"Jack, go long just like at home," Sam ordered.

"Except you've never hit that pass in your life. I'll go short in the flat," Jack countered.

Jogging in the flat, Jack caught Sam's pass. As Jack trotted toward the sideline, Jenna caught him from behind and jumped on his back. She wrapped her arms around his neck and brought her feet together around his waist. Being a good sport, Jack collapsed and went down with Jenna on top of him. Jenna maintained her hold on him as he lay on his stomach. Enjoying the moment, she grazed her face on the back of his neck and moved her lips up to his ear. Jack felt her warmth and chills ran up his spine.

"Jack," she said.

"Yeah," he answered, not being able to see her.

"You smell good," she whispered.

"You, too," he said, assuming she did.

As the exchange went on, the others started yelling at the couple to break it up.

Jenna sensed their displeasure and pushed herself off of Jack. She proceeded to step on him on the way back to her huddle. Jenna was so petite the gesture made Jack laugh to himself.

Every time Jack touched the ball, Jenna tackled him. Every time he lay on the ground, she made a comment or touched him in a way that made him want her. He was becoming so worked up that he finally had to leave the game. He claimed he was tired but the tension was becoming too great. Jack liked Jenna tremendously but he convinced himself he was committed to Wendy. He couldn't possibly dishonor her, especially in public.

"Where are you going, Jack?" Sam called to his brother as he walked from the field.

"I'm going to take a break," Jack yelled back. "Anyone want to join me?"

Jack pulled up a chair and pretty soon everyone left the field to join him. It wasn't two minutes after they sat down before Tim had an idea.

"Anyone want to go swimming?" Tim asked.

"Are you kidding?" Jack retorted, "It's the middle of November."

"It's okay, buddy," Tim laughed. "The pool's heated and I'm sure there's an extra pair of trunks in the pool house you could use."

Victoria slammed her drink on the table and said, "I worked up a pretty good sweat from the game. I'm in."

Acting as if it were the middle of summer, Jenna added, "Me, too."

Hannah, Moriah, and Sarah all stood up and the five girls proceeded to strip down right then and there.

When Jenna unbuttoned her pants, Jack's eyes almost popped out of their sockets. All the boys were mesmerized by what was happening. At this point, Jenna and her friends had the attention of everyone at the party.

When Jenna unzipped her jeans, Jack could see red immediately and became enthralled. When she started to shake her pants down around her hips, he sat up in anticipation of bare skin. When her pants were completely down, she yanked off her sweatshirt revealing a matching top. That's when Jack and the boys realized that Jenna and the rest of the girls had worn bikini swimsuits under their clothes.

"What's going on here?" Jack said, pointing at Tim. "You got us good. We thought . . . you know what we thought. They knew we were going swimming the whole time."

"Man, you should have seen your faces. I thought you guys were going to faint," Tim said with a smirk.

"Anyone going to join us?" Jenna asked, directing her question to Jack.

Jenna had an awesome figure. She was curvy, tight, and muscular all at the same time. She let her hair down and it fell on her shoulders. She was beautiful and Jack wanted her more now than ever. Her red bikini attracted Jack like a matador cape attracts a bull.

"I am," Jack answered, racing for the pool house.

Pretty soon the pool was full of teenagers having the time of their lives. When Tim ran out of spare bathing suits, people started jumping in with their clothes on. The party goers spent the rest of the afternoon in the pool.

Later on, near dusk, when most of the guests had departed, only Tim, Jack, Sam, Victoria, Sarah, and Jenna remained. Tim, Victoria, Sam, and Sarah all suddenly decided to get out of the water and retire to the pool house while Jack and Jenna stayed behind in the pool.

"Finally alone," Jenna said, as she swam over to Jack.

Jack reached out for her and pulled her against his massive torso. The heat created between their bodies made Jack yearn for her. With their faces only inches apart, Jack and Jenna stared into each other's eyes wondering what to do next. They

137

could see each other's desire to further the moment and they began kissing.

Seconds later, Jenna pulled back. "Aren't you forgetting something?"

"What? Does my breath smell? I'll get a mint," Jack joked, knowing all too well what Jenna was referring to.

"Wendy," Jenna said, right before she gave Jack another passionate kiss.

After recovering from the kiss, Jack rolled his eyes and responded, "Oh yeah. It's alright. I broke up with her."

"Since when?" Jenna asked while she wrapped her legs around Jack's waist.

"Since right now. I just haven't told her yet," Jack smiled.

"Okay then," Jenna said as the two embraced.

"Caught you!" Tim shouted from the doorway of the pool house.

"Did not," Jack answered back.

"Did, too," Victoria, Sam, and Sarah yelled out of the house.

"You guys are busted," Tim laughed, walking past as the couple climbed out of the pool.

"Jenna, I think you owe me ten bucks," Tim said in a matter of fact tone.

"Not now," Jenna whispered through her clinched teeth.

"Why do you owe him ten dollars?" Jack asked Jenna, trying to figure out the deal.

"We made a little wager," Tim began.

"Are you crazy?" Jenna scolded Tim. "There is no way I'm paying you if you don't stop talking right now."

Pausing briefly to think of how much the money meant to him, Tim continued. "We made a bet and I won. I said I could have you guys together by tonight if she agreed to do everything I said. The football game, the bikinis, the works. She agreed and I won. Now pay up, you little hussy."

"I'm going to kill you," Jenna growled as she lunged for Tim.

Jack grabbed her arm and pulled her toward him. "It's okay. I'm not upset...I'm happy. This is the nicest thing anyone has ever done for me. I've always known how great you are. I was just too stupid not to have done anything about it. I think I'm in love with you."

"What?" Tim gasped. "This has to be worth at least twenty dollars."

Chapter 12

"Out of all the teams in NFL history, who do you think is the best?" Jack asked Sam from across the living room.

"I think the 49ers were the best of all time. Montana and Rice were the best combination in the history of football. They dominated the '80s like no one ever has," Sam proclaimed.

"What about the Cowboys in the '90s? Aikman, Smith, and Irvin were pretty awesome." Jack countered.

The only Dallas Cowboys I remember you seeing were the Dallas Cowboy cheerleaders on that calendar in your dresser drawer," Sam joked.

Jack didn't think that was funny at all and jumped up from the sofa and pulled Sam to the floor. Within three seconds, Sam was on his stomach with Jack putting his elbow into Sam's back. Luckily for Sam, their parents were just returning from the supermarket and Jack had to retreat before they walked into the house.

"We'll continue this discussion at a later time," Jack insisted as he retook his seat.

"Yes, I think that would be wise," Sam snickered, straightening his clothes and hair before letting his mother in the front door.

The game was well into the second half and the Patriots were dominating the Packers. The Bowdens had a tradition of watching the full game regardless of the score. The boys' conversation, however, drifted from the Patriots to their own team.

"After we win Homecoming this week, we'll have to start playing better if we want to win state," Jack predicted.

"I know," Sam agreed. "We certainly have caught some breaks in the tight games."

"I hope Chuck can be a little more consistent through the playoffs," Jack wondered aloud. "It's crazy how he can set the world on fire one game and come back and be the world's worst quarterback the next game."

"You don't think that's a coincidence, do you Jack?" Sam quizzed.

"What do you mean?" Jack asked, confused by Sam's implication.

"What do you mean, what do I mean?" Sam answered.

"Stop that. What are you trying to say?" Jack asked in frustration.

"I'm saying, Chuck is playing the spread," Sam explained. "He's gambling on our football games. Sometimes he's shaving points and other times he's running up the score. How else can you explain all of the boneheaded plays he's made? He walks off the field with a smile and shows no regret. Then some games, he scores points like his life depends on it. Something is going on. I know it."

"That's ridiculous," Jack countered. "No one gambles on high school football games."

"You are so naïve, Jack. Come over here and take a look at this," Sam instructed.

Sam walked over to his computer and did a quick internet search and was able to pull up two sites within seconds that took bets on high school football games. Sacred Heart was favored by thirty-one over Cumberland this Friday in the homecoming game.

"Holy Bejesus! That's insane. We'll be 9-0 when we enter the playoffs," Jack said in reaction to the line.

"We haven't won that game yet," Sam replied.

Both boys just stood and stared at the screen thinking about the possibility that Chuck was actually gambling on the games.

"If you were Chuck, assuming you are right, how would you bet this week's game?" Jack inquired of Sam.

"I'd take Cumberland and the points. Thirty-one is hard to cover and a quarterback can easily affect the score by a touchdown or two either way. We'll have to wait and see how Chuck reacts. Then we'll know how he bet the game." Then as an afterthought, Sam said in relief, "at least we won't have to worry about losing. With a thirty-one point spread, Chuck won't have to put the game in jeopardy."

Jack thought about Sam's last statement and said, "We shouldn't say anything. We need Chuck to play well in the playoffs to win the championship. If we could get some evidence against Chuck, we could blackmail him into doing whatever we want."

"We could break into his house and go through his stuff," Sam proposed.

"No, we can't do anything illegal."

"What if I hacked into his bank account? We could track his transactions. That might give us some clues."

"Illegal."

"What about phone taps?"

"Phone taps? You don't have any phone taps. C'mon, think harder."

"I know," declared Sam. "We could go through his trash. I saw it on TV. Once it's on the curb, it's not illegal anymore. TV cops are always going through someone's trash."

In a sarcastic tone Jack said, "That's a great idea. You should definitely go through his trash. Tell me about it when you're done."

"You know what you should do right now?" Sam asked with a straight face.

"No, what?"

"You should call up Wendy and tell her how much you missed her yesterday?" Sam said in the spirit of making fun.

Unfortunately for Sam, Jack stopped laughing and jumped on top of him. Wrestling Sam to the floor, Jack smashed his face into the carpet.

"That's great advice. You got any other good ideas while we're discussing it?"

"Yes," answered Sam in a muffled tone. "Can you please get off of me? I'm getting rug burn on my face."

*

When Jack entered the chemistry classroom, Jenna was already in her seat. She had her head down and was writing in her notebook. Jack scanned the room and saw Tim and Victoria looking at him as he sat next to Jenna. After Jack took his seat, Jenna looked up at him and smiled. There was no time to talk because Mr. Cain was already beginning the lesson.

While Mr. Cain lectured on the number of valence electrons in group seventeen elements, Jack could not help but think about Jenna. It had been almost two days since he proclaimed his love for her and he had barely said hi to her. He felt like two people in love should be spending time together, not time apart. He knew he wanted to be with her instead of Wendy, but he still had the business of breaking up with Wendy before he could commence his relationship with Jenna.

As he sat there dwelling on the impending confrontation with Wendy, Jack couldn't help but notice Jenna's overwhelming beauty. He wondered if she was always this irresistible or was he just blind to it before? He had talked to her dozens of times in the past, but now he didn't know what to say. The longer the silence existed between them, the more difficult it became.

At long last, the lecture was over and lab portion of class began. When Jack and Jenna moved to the lab station, Jack couldn't hold back any longer.

"Hey Jenna, how's it going?"

"Fine, you?" Jenna replied almost ignoring the tension in Jack's voice.

Jenna proceeded to gather the materials for the lab without feeling a need to help Jack along with the conversation.

Jack cut to the chase, "I think we should go out."

"On a date?" Jenna asked.

"Many dates," Jack clarified.

Jenna turned to Jack and flipped her hair out of her face. Smiling she said, "That's a great idea." Then the smile faded. "I don't think Wendy will be too happy about it," she added with a pouty frown.

Jack became tongue-tied. He didn't have a response for that.

Mercifully, Jenna rescued him. "Look, I know how things were Saturday. I took advantage of you. If you go back with Wendy, I won't blame you. You don't owe me anything. I had a great time Saturday and I don't have any regrets."

Jack thought for a minute and then reaffirmed his position, "I meant what I said Saturday."

"It was in the heat of the moment, Jack," Jenna said, trying to give Jack an out.

"I admit, you were rockin' that bathing suit, but it was all true," Jack blushed. "Give me a week. I'll take care of Wendy and then we can be together."

"Okay," Jenna shrugged.

As an afterthought, Jack asked, "Do you want to go to the homecoming dance with me?"

"Only if I win homecoming queen," Jenna smiled.

Reaching into his shirt pocket, he pulled out the ballot he had received during homeroom and handed it to Jenna.

Jenna unfolded the slip of paper. Jack had drawn a devil's fork next to Wendy's name and a halo next to hers. He had checked her name with XOXO.

Laughing, Jenna handed the paper back to Jack and said, "Okay, I'll go to the dance with you either way."

*

Just like every other Monday, Tim and Mark ate lunch with Jack.

"Do you think Wendy knows about Saturday?" Tim asked Jack.

"I don't know, maybe. You know how news travels around this place. If she doesn't know already, it would be some sort of a miracle," Jack answered through a bite of his burger. "I kind of wish she did find out. It would take the burden off of me having to tell her. I'm kind of dreading it. How do you break up with someone like her? She might punch me in the nose or run me over with my own car."

"We should role-play," offered Mark. "I'll be Wendy and you be . . . well, you." Pausing for affect, Mark pulled his hair back and imitated Wendy. "Hi, Jack. Would you polish my shoes, before you walk my dog and do my homework?"

Jack laughed and then thought for a moment, "Listen, you ungrateful little tramp. I'm tired of your bony ass walking all over me and everyone else. We're through! You can pick your stuff up off my front lawn."

Mark smirked, "That won't happen in a million years. Nobody is as much a hard ass as Wendy."

"Holy crap! Here she comes," Tim announced, looking the other way.

Walking up to the table, Wendy addressed Tim and Mark, "Good morning Larry and Moe. Where's Curly?"

Mark took exception to "The Three Stooges" reference and answered back, "Guess who's not going to win homecoming queen?"

Mark stood up and said to Tim, "C'mon, let's get out of here. I don't want to be collateral damage."

Jack knew what he meant but Wendy just had a confused look on her face when they left.

Shaking her head, Wendy turned to Jack and said, "I missed you this weekend. How was the party, Saturday?"

Jack couldn't tell whether she already knew about Jenna or if she was truly interested in his weekend. "It was fine."

Before Wendy could ask any more questions, Jack looked at his watch and said, "Say Wendy, I've only got a couple of minutes left before class. We should get together tonight."

"Yes. I was just going to ask you if wanted to double with Chuck and Sue. It's Sue's birthday and we wanted to do something to celebrate."

Jack threw his head back. This was becoming more painful than ever. Not only did he have to break up with her, which would put his life in danger, but now he had to spend the evening with Chuck Cruise.

"C'mon Wendy, you know I don't get along with Chuck. Can't we just spend the evening alone?" Jack begged.

"If you do this one thing for me, I won't ask you for anything ever again."

That statement was over the top. Wendy not asking for anything for five minutes was a stretch. Ever again was impossible. She knew about Jenna and Jack knew she knew. It had all become a game. Jack decided to play along. Just one more night and he would be rid of Wendy forever.

*

Jack wanted to drive so he could maintain some type of control over the evening, but Wendy exerted her power and soon he was riding in the back of Chuck's car. In the back seat of his most hated rival's car, with a girl he now detested, on a Monday night, Jack couldn't think of a worse scenario.

"Where are we going?" Jack asked without inflection.

"Liquor store and then to the beach," Wendy informed Jack.

With the music blasting, Chuck pulled up to Appanoug Liquor Store. He stopped the car and turned around to Jack. Handing him two twenty dollar bills, he said, "I want three sixes of Budweiser. Make sure you get the cold ones."

Accepting the bills, Jack objected. "I can't buy beer. I'm not twenty-one."

"C'mon Jack," Wendy urged, "You look twenty-one. Just try."

"I'll buy yours if you go get it," Chuck added.

With all three of the teenagers encouraging him to make an attempt, Jack eventually agreed and exited the car. He looked back and three of them smiled and watched intently as he went up the sidewalk.

Walking to the back of the store where he could hear the coolers, Jack located the beer. After ensuring the beer was truly chilled, Jack brought up a case of beer to the counter.

When he took out the money to pay for the beer, the cashier asked, "Identification, please?"

Jack patted down his pants and shrugged his shoulders. "I must have left my wallet back at the house."

"Sorry. No ID, no beer."

Just as Jack was about to leave the store empty handed, a police car pulled up to the front of the store with its lights on. Two uniformed cops got out and walked into the store.

"Excuse me, sir," barked the big cop. "We just received a call that minors are attempting to purchase alcohol at this store."

The clerk just shrugged his shoulders and said, "This gentleman is the only person that has been in here for the last twenty minutes and he can't produce any identification."

"What's your name, son?" asked the second cop.

"Jack Bowden."

"How old are you, son?"

"Seventeen."

"You're going to have to come down to the station with us," the big cop said, putting his hand on Jack's shoulder.

The cops escorted Jack to the squad car parked on the curb next to the entrance. When Jack came through the door, he could see Chuck and Wendy watching as he was being taken away. He thought they would follow him to the police station but they didn't. When the police car took a left at the intersection, Jack turned around and watched as Chuck's car headed off in the opposite direction.

The ride was short and soon Jack was being led to a cell in the rear of the building. The officer didn't say anything when he locked the door and Jack didn't feel like asking any questions. When he was alone, he moved over to the cot and sat down. He closed his eyes, hung his head and contemplated his future.

His head spun. He thought about his parents. What would they think? Would they be ashamed of him? Would they be embarrassed? What kind of punishment would he get for something like this? The questions wouldn't stop.

Then there was school and the football team. Would he get suspended from school or perhaps kicked off the football team? Colleges would find out he had a police record and his scholarship opportunities would evaporate. Father Joseph might even cancel his weekly performances at Friday Mass.

Nothing good was coming of this event. Jack was reduced to mental anguish. He thought about all of the people that depended on him. He couldn't believe that he could make such a stupid mistake. Maybe he wasn't perfect, but this was certainly not who he was.

Jack laid on the cot and negative thoughts raced through his mind. He had let everyone down and now, not only was he going to have to suffer, everyone else associated with him would be impacted as well. The strain of the events was overtaking him. He felt sick. His stomach was queasy and his head pounded. He could barely think. Tears rolled out of his eyes and down his face.

Feeling helpless and totally out of control, Jack decided to pray. He prayed that his mother would forgive him. He prayed that his teammates would forgive him, and he even prayed that his brother would forgive him. After an hour, his penance was interrupted by a familiar voice.

"Hey loser! You alright?"

Jack looked up and there stood Jenna holding onto the bars with both hands.

"I've come to bail you out," Jenna giggled, "but it's going to cost you."

"How can you bail me out?" Jack wanted to know, wiping the moisture from his face

"My dad is the Chief of Police. He said I could get you out if you come over to our house and watch Monday Night Football. What do you say?"

"Are you freaking kidding? The freaking Chief of Police wants me to watch Monday Night Football at your house?"

Within minutes, Jack was riding with Jenna to her house. "I thought I was dead and buried. This is unbelievable. How did you find out I'd been arrested?"

"My dad heard it on the scanner. He told the cops on duty to hold you until I was ready to pick you up."

"What about the charges?" Jack asked. "Are there any charges? What about my parents? Did they call them? They're going to kill me."

"There aren't any charges and there's no record of this ever happening. The police didn't even call your parents," Jenna informed Jack.

Jack's fortune could not have turned any quicker. Crushed and miserable, his burden had been liberated just as quickly. He thanked God under his breath and vowed never to dishonor his family and friends again.

Jack sighed, "I *am* the luckiest person alive."

"Not exactly. There was one phone call made tonight. Apparently, a cell phone registered to Janice Thompson made an anonymous 911 call about some minors buying liquor at Appanoug Liquor Store. That call was made four minutes before you were picked up."

"Oh, my God! Janice Thompson is Wendy's mother," Jack grimaced. "That means it must have been Wendy who made the call. Wow! This is truly unbelievable. I've never known anyone who would stoop so low. She must have been really pissed when she found out about us on Saturday."

"I've heard of boyfriends being put in the doghouse," Jenna remarked as she squeezed Jack's hand, "but I've never heard of them being put in the jailhouse."

Chapter 13

Mr. Witherspoon excused himself and went to bed. Finally, alone with Jenna, Jack reclined on the sofa and reached into the bowl of popcorn. On the other side of the bowl, Jenna watched the game intently, listening to the announcer's analysis of the Giant's defensive strategy.

"I think the Giants should bring in their safeties. The 49ers aren't going to throw the ball until the Giants stop the run. With the injuries they have at linebacker, it's just not going to happen."

"That guy should keep his mouth shut," Jenna said, objecting to his conclusions. "Even my mom knows the 49ers don't run on every play. They'll throw on the next down."

The 49ers ran play action and threw a pass down the sideline for fifteen yards.

"What'd I tell you?" Jenna said proudly as if she should be the Giant's defensive coordinator.

She looked at Jack for confirmation and he supported her. "You were right. I knew you were right before they ran the play. I'd have said so but my mouth was full."

Jenna grabbed a handful of popcorn and threw it at Jack. "Don't patronize me. You can say what you think."

"I've got a question," Jack said, changing the subject. "How did you find out it was Wendy that got me busted?"

"When my dad heard the dispatcher send the cops, he became curious. There has never been a 911 call for teenagers buying beer before. So he called Emergency Services. They said the caller just gave the information and hung up without giving their name or anything. That's when he requested the trace."

"I sure was lucky tonight. If I had been arrested, I probably would have been suspended from the football team."

Moving the popcorn onto the end table, Jenna slid close to Jack. "Or we wouldn't be together tonight, watching this exciting football game."

Becoming aware of Jenna's proximity, Jacks lips moved within an inch of hers. "Or we wouldn't be kissing like this," Jack whispered.

The couple wrapped their arms around each other and began kissing. Their passion was so intense, time seemed to stand still. They were enjoying each other so much neither of them saw the Giants come back to the beat the 49ers in the last two minutes.

*

"How cool is that?" Jack said to Mark upon telling him the story of being picked up, jailed, and then rescued.

"What are you going to do to Wendy?" Mark asked, hoping for something evil and horrific.

"Nothing."

"What?" Mark objected. "She deserves to be punished."

"No. It's not my style. I just want to move on."

"Don't look now. Here she comes."

Out of the chaos of students getting ready for another school day, Wendy and Sue appeared and approached Jack and Mark.

Wendy didn't hug or touch Jack. Instead, she kept her distance.

"Jack, I'm real sorry about last night," Wendy began. "We got scared when the cops showed up. You understand, right?"

Jack looked at Mark and then turned his attention back to Wendy.

"It's okay, Wendy. It's probably the nicest thing you've ever done for me."

"What are you talking about?" Wendy replied not understanding how going to jail was a pleasant experience.

"Because you called the cops, I didn't have to spend the night with you or Chuck. I really couldn't be happier."

"I didn't call the cops," Wendy lied. She glanced at Sue with a quizzical look of dismay.

"It's alright. I know what happened and everything worked out for the best," Jack consoled.

Wendy could see that Jack was pulling away from her emotionally and she was determined to win his forgiveness. "It was Chuck's idea. I swear. He made me do it."

Wendy began to cry and Jack stayed silent. "I'm sorry, Jack. I didn't know what I was doing. Please forgive me."

Jack knew Wendy too well. If he forgave her, they would be right back to where they were two weeks ago.

Jack broke the silence. "We can still be friends."

"Friends? I don't want to be friends!" Wendy shouted, becoming hysterical. "You can't break up with me three days before Homecoming. I'm going to be queen and you have to be there to support me. I can't go to Homecoming alone."

Wendy started to cry again and Sue turned to hug her. Wendy was sobbing in Sue's arms and Jack and Mark were frozen in place.

"I understand how you feel the way you do, but I just can't go out with you anymore," Jack said in a hushed voice. "You did try to get me arrested and ruin my life."

After another heart stopping thirty seconds, Wendy composed herself.

"You're making a huge mistake. I'm the hottest girl you'll ever date and no matter how much you want me back, I'll never take you back. I'll never speak to you again."

Then in a huff, Wendy spun and the two girls walked the other way.

Goose pimples ran up and down Jack's arms as a feeling of elation passed over him. He was free. He was free from Wendy and free to pursue Jenna. This feeling was rare and he paused to enjoy the moment.

Jack turned to Mark and asked, "We'll always be friends, right?"

"You'll always be my friend." Mark laughed. "Nothing could ever come between us. Not a nuclear warhead or even a girl named Wendy Thompson."

*

Jack walked into chemistry with his head in the clouds. He couldn't wait to tell Jenna what had happened. Jenna was already in her seat and beamed with joy when she saw Jack come in. He wanted to walk right up to her and kiss her but he felt like the entire class was watching him.

He sat down next to her, leaned over and whispered into her ear, "I've got big news."

"That's terrific, but I've got bigger news," Jenna countered, smiling from ear to ear.

Jack sensed a challenge and continued, "My extremely large news will surpass your news any day."

"My news is extensive, vast, enormous, huge, and nothing, I repeat nothing, you could think of in one million years could be bigger than my big news," Jenna proclaimed. "Top that, Jack Bowden!"

"My news is infinitely large. And nothing beats infinity."

"Except infinity to the infinite power," Jenna asserted, making her head move from side to side with her lips puffed out.

Jenna's reluctance to give in told Jack that her news was indeed bigger and better.

"Okay, what's your big news?" Jack asked in defeat.

"Smaller news always goes first," Jenna announced.

"Brace yourself," Jack paused. "I broke up with Wendy."

"That is excellent news, Jack," Jenna remarked, "but I already knew that. So technically, it's not really news."

"Okay, miss smarty pants, what's your big news?" Jack asked.

"Get ready, Jack."

"I'm ready."

"No. Hold onto the desk. I don't want you to fall on the floor."

"Just tell me."

"My dad is bringing a friend to Friday's game. He's the head recruiter for the Nebraska State Mustangs football team."

Jack paused with his mouth open then exclaimed, "Holy freakin' mother of God!"

Jack immediately quieted his voice and asked, "Why is he coming?"

"He's coming to see you play, stupid head. If you're good enough, he might offer you a scholarship," Jenna revealed.

"Does anyone else know?"

"It wouldn't be news if anyone did, now would it?" Jenna answered in a muffled tone. Then she added, "There's more."

"More?"

"Yes, more. It means additional information is coming."

"Yes, that's what it means," Jack said, wondering if he'd ever had more fun conversing with a girl in his life.

"My dad and his friend are flying us to the Nebraska State game on Saturday."

"Oh my God!" Jack called out much to Mr. Cain's displeasure. "You're right. Your news was bigger than mine. This is awesome."

Jack sat back in his seat and felt a euphoric feeling of happiness overcome him. He stared down at his textbook but he couldn't see the words. He could only envision himself at the Nebraska State game.

Jack waited a minute for the shock to subside. He looked back over to Jenna and found Jenna smiling at him. He didn't know how to show gratitude for such wonderful gifts.

He merely mouthed the words, "Thank you" to her.

She returned the gesture with, "You're welcome."

*

The street was dark and the houses were well lit. The Firebird purred as the car rolled forward toward Chuck's house. It was Thursday, trash night, and two big containers sat curbside.

"I'll stop and you get out and grab the bags out of the trash. Throw them in the trunk and we'll open them up at Tim's house," Jack instructed Sam and Tim.

Like seasoned sanitation workers, the boys had the trash in seconds and the car sped off, leaving the containers rocking in their wake.

"I sure hope they have a garbage disposal," Tim grumbled. "If I have to stick my hands in some three day old chicken carcass, I'll puke."

"All new houses have one," Sam suspected. "I brought gloves anyway."

The boys speculated on what they might find.

"What if we find dirty diapers?" Sam asked.

"Chuck's a little old to be wearing diapers," Jack half joked.

"I don't know," Tim said, expressing uncertainty. "He's a big baby if you ask me."

With the car safely in the garage, the boys removed the three bags of trash and opened them up on a large plastic drop cloth. The boys spread the trash out as thin as possible. They stood over it wondering where to begin.

"Try to sort the trash by piles," Sam began. "Let's put all of the kitchen trash back into the bags. We need to look for stuff that has writing on it."

"Look at all of these liquor bottles," Tim observed. "You think they would recycle all of this glass."

"They probably don't want the neighbors finding out," Sam deduced. "Imagine the rumors?"

"When you think about it, there's not that much trash here. We have five bags a week and there are only four of us," Jack commented.

"Is it just Chuck and his mother?" Tim asked.

"I think," Jack guessed.

"I guess they really like microwave dinners. There's like, twelve boxes and hardly any other food containers," Tim remarked.

"You've got to feel a little sorry for him," Jack sympathized. "I look forward to dinner every night. It's my favorite part of the day."

After sorting the garbage, the boys were able to concentrate on a small pile of bills, notes, and printouts they had collected.

"Look at these lottery tickets. I think we're on to something," Sam concluded.

"Lottery tickets…that doesn't mean anything," Jack moaned. "Dad buys lottery tickets every week."

"Yeah, but he doesn't buy them in Connecticut," Tim declared as he snatched them from Sam pointing to a casino's emblem on the back.

"Jackpot!" Sam cried. "Look, sports book receipts from the casino. I knew it! I knew he was betting the games."

"Give me that," Jack ordered. "These are college games. That's not our games. That's not proof."

"C'mon Jack. That's good enough," Sam whined. "It's called a pattern of evidence. I saw it on TV. Let's at least go to the coach and tell him."

"What? Are you kidding?" Jack asked, clearly objecting. "What are we going to tell him? We went through Chuck's trash? No. We should go directly to Chuck and confront him. We'll get what we want that way."

"What do we want?" Sam pondered.

"To win, you knucklehead," Jack said, flicking him in the ear.

*

Jack and the defense surrounded Chuck at his locker and Jack stepped to the front. Chuck became frightened at the sight of Jack Bowden wearing his most serious face. Having learned that Jack knew of Wendy's 911 call, Chuck figured that Jack would want to clear the air about his participation.

Chuck stood and still had to look up to meet Jack's angry stare.

Poking Chuck in the chest with an iron like index finger, Jack called Chuck out, "Let's step outside."

Becoming noticeably nervous, sweat appeared on Chuck's brow.

"I know what you're thinking, Jack, but it's different. It was all Wendy. I didn't even know she was going to call the police and she did it before I had a chance to stop her."

"Outside!" Jack ordered, poking him with such great force he fell back into his locker.

Chuck took a few steps toward the locker room exit. Looking back over his shoulder, he hoped someone would notice the danger he was in. The throng of bodies following him was so thick that neither Matt nor Billy knew what was happening.

Once outside, the defense formed a circle around Jack and Chuck.

Chuck began to plead for mercy. "C'mon Jack, it's not worth this. Nothing even happened. You, yourself, admitted that it was the best thing that ever happened to you. Didn't you say that to Wendy? Please, Jack. Give me a break here, will you? You know how Wendy can make you do things you don't want to do. She made me drive off...she made me."

Chuck's last statement struck Jack. That part was true. Wendy did have a way about making you do things you didn't want to do, but he wasn't here to fight Chuck about that anyway.

Shaking his head, trying to pry Wendy from his thoughts, he addressed Chuck. "Relax, will you? I'm not going to beat you up . . . today, maybe another time, but not today."

"Then what? What's this all about?"

"We want to talk to you about your gambling problem."

"What gambling problem?" Chuck asked, looking around at all of the disbelieving faces.

"The one where we lose the state championship game because you get your butt in a sling...that gambling problem," Jack barked. "The one where you put yourself before the team. The one you're going to clean up right now or we'll beat you to a bloody pulp."

Chuck realized they knew, but he still maintained his innocence. "I don't bet on our games. I swear I don't."

"We think that you do, Chuck!" Jack roared. Jack thrust his clenched hands into Chuck's chest, sending him to the ground. Jack stood over Chuck and pointed sternly down at him and gave him an ultimatum. "If you screw us, we'll kick your ass."

Chapter 14

The temperature had dropped significantly. November was always cold in Rhode Island, but this Friday night was finger-numbingly bitter. As the players huddled around Coach Dawson, each player exhaled a cloud of condensed vapor. While the Screaming Eagles were favored to win this game easily, the cold weather had a tendency to slow everyone down a step or two.

Sacred Heart kicked to Cumberland to open the game. The Cumberland Clippers began their first series at their own twenty-one.

Well aware the Nebraska State recruiter was in the grandstand, Jack was full of energy. He was determined to make a lasting impression. With Sam working his magic, the Sacred Heart defense went to work. Sam called the play and the Screaming Eagles attacked at full speed.

On first down, Cumberland went to a pro set with split backs. Sam read the pass as a deep post. With double coverage on the intended receiver and the back in the flat blanketed, Jack blitzed the quarterback and crushed him for an eight yard loss.

Jack was all business. While his teammates were celebrating their first down victory, Jack was already thinking about second down.

On second and eighteen, the Clippers called a screen pass. Jack identified the targeted receiver and spied him all the way. When he snuck in the left zone, Jack followed. The quarterback drifted back under a heavy pass rush. When the ball floated out to the receiver, Jack accelerated and hit the receiver just as the ball arrived. The force of the tackle knocked the ball loose for an incomplete pass. The receiver lay motionless on the field and the Cumberland trainer ran to attend to him.

After a three minute delay, the injured player regained his feet and walked gingerly to the sideline. On third and eighteen, Cumberland tried a deep out and the ball sailed harmlessly out of bounds.

Jack and the defense trotted off the field to a thunderous applause from the home crowd. When the players removed their helmets, ten of the eleven faces were painted with jubilation, but not Jack. The first series was merely an introduction to what was to follow. He gathered his defense on the bench and made adjustments for the next series. His teammates adopted his demeanor and the defense became serious and focused.

The Screaming Eagles' offense struck quickly. On the fifth play of their opening drive, Singleton bounced off left tackle and scored the first touchdown. With only six minutes gone in the first quarter, Sacred Heart led 7-0.

Feeding off the momentum, the defense took the game into overdrive. Cumberland tried to run on first down up the middle. Jack and three others stuffed it for no gain. On second down, Jack shed two blockers before tackling the quarterback on an option play. On third down, Mark and Jack combined on another quarterback sack for a loss of eleven. Again, Cumberland was forced to punt.

The defense watched the offense march right down the field. Chuck was hitting everything he threw. He threw to Tanner for fifteen, to Singleton for eleven and then to Shaffer for thirty. The offense punched it in on a quarterback sneak and the rout was on.

By halftime, the Screaming Eagles were up 42-0. Jack had made eight unassisted tackles, forced a fumble, and was easily handling two blockers on almost every play. Even Chuck was having an outstanding game. He had thrown for three touchdowns and had run for another.

During halftime of the homecoming game, the Sacred Heart team normally retired to the locker room, leaving only the captains behind to crown the queen and her court. However, because the game was so out of hand, the entire team stayed on the sideline for the ceremony.

Jack approached Chuck right before the entrance of the candidates.

"Nice game, Chuck," Jack acknowledged. "Keep up the good work."

"Thanks," Chuck responded, wanting to keep his distance.

"Listen. I've got a problem and I need your help," Jack began. "When this whole homecoming thing started, I was dating Wendy and now I'm with Jenna."

"So," Chuck interrupted.

"So, we practiced this with me escorting Wendy. I'm supposed to give Wendy flowers and the crown if she wins."

"So what do you want from me?" Chuck asked.

"I need you to switch with me. You had Jenna and I need you to take Wendy."

"No way!" Chuck protested.

"C'mon, Chuck. After what you did to me. I'll call it even." Jack proposed.

"Okay, I'll do it, but Wendy's going to freak."

"That's what I expect," Jack admitted.

When the three queen candidates entered the field area, there was a pathway for the girls to parade through before they met their escort halfway between the sideline and the center of the field. Luckily for Jack, Jenna was the first candidate to walk down the path. Jack approached her and fell right in step with her. Reaching with her right arm, Jenna slipped it through the underside of Jack's elbow.

Smiling, Jenna said, "This is a nice surprise."

Not looking at Jenna, Jack responded without moving his lips, "I thought it was the right thing to do under the circumstances."

The couple walked to midfield and Jack took his place behind Jenna.

When Chuck met Wendy, she was seething. Her stern expression scared both Jack and Jenna. As she moved closer, she glared at them but did not say anything before taking her place on the field.

Once Kelly and Matt were in place, the public address announcer began. "Thank you ladies and gentlemen. Tonight, we crown this year's Sacred Heart Homecoming Queen. But first let me introduce the candidates and their escorts. First, Jenna Witherspoon accompanied by Chuck Cruise."

A murmur buzzed through the crowd because they all recognized that it was Jack standing alongside Jenna and not Chuck.

The PA announcer continued reading his script. "Second, Wendy Thompson escorted by Jack Bowden."

Wendy waved and Chuck raised his hand, chuckling to himself from behind.

"Third, Kelly Singer escorted by Matt Singleton." The PA announcer paused and then began again. "The candidates were nominated by the football team and then voted on by the student body. This year's Sacred Heart Homecoming Queen is . . . Jenna Witherspoon."

The crowd cheered loudly and the band struck up the school song. The student council representatives gave Jack the flowers and the crown. Taking first the crown, Jack placed the tiara atop Jenna's head. He then handed her the flowers, gave her a kiss on the cheek, before stepping aside so the crowd could see their new queen.

When Chuck handed Wendy her consolation flowers, she lost control. In a fit of rage, she took the flowers and ran five steps over to Jenna and swung her flowers like a baseball bat. Unsuspecting, Jenna was blindsided. When the flowers hit her in the face, they exploded. Knocked back by the flowers, but not down, Jenna staggered away putting her arms up. Wendy threw down the stems and charged at Jenna, but Jack stepped between the two girls and stopped Wendy in her tracks.

Thrashing about like a crazy woman, Wendy screamed, "First, you stole my boyfriend, now you're stealing my crown!"

Jenna was so embarrassed, she put her hands in front of her face and began to cry.

Wendy continued her verbal onslaught. "I hate you, you bitch! I hate you!"

Holding Wendy back, Jack decided he couldn't let this continue. He proceeded to pick Wendy up over his shoulder and he carried her off the field kicking and screaming. Because he was wearing his uniform, he couldn't feel Wendy's punches through his shoulder pads.

When he neared the sidelines, the shocked crowd, who was deafly silent through the unruly event, began to cheer for Jack as he carried Wendy out of the stadium. Thankfully for Jack, Wendy's parents met him at the gate and were able to take her from him. Jack returned to the field to a greater cheer than before.

Jogging out onto the field, Jack embraced Jenna. The two hugged while fifteen hundred people watched and wondered what would happen next.

"What am I supposed to do now?" Jenna asked Jack so only he could hear.

Jack whispered in her ear, "Smile and pretend the whole thing didn't happen. You're their queen. Everybody loves you."

"Even you, Jack?"

"Mostly me," Jack assured her.

They separated and faced the crowd for an even greater round of applause.

*

In the locker room after the game, Jack and the others were getting dressed for the homecoming dance. Nearly ready, Jack only needed to put on his tie and shoes.

Mark, who had just had the tape cut from his ankles, sat down next to Jack. "You're in a little bit of a hurry to get to the dance, aren't you?"

"You would be too if your date was the queen," Jack answered back.

"Nice game tonight," Mark commented. "You were on fire. I've never seen you that intense. What did you have, like twenty tackles?"

"Yeah, I was hoping for a turnover or something," Jack responded. "Nebraska State was here tonight."

"That's what I heard," Mark said, stripping off his shoulder pads.

"Who told you?" Jack asked, thinking only he had known.

"Sam."

"I'm going to kill him. He can't keep his mouth shut for one minute."

"Hold on, Jack. He was just trying to help. He figured that if everyone took the game seriously, then we would all play better."

Thinking for a minute, Jack presumed his brother was right. "I'm sorry. I thought it was something I wasn't supposed to tell anyone."

"How about Chuck?" Mark changed the subject. "He played great tonight. If he plays like that in the playoffs, we'll be unstoppable."

"Verdict is still out on that one," Jack commented, buffing his shoes. "He might have given the thirty-one points and still won on this game. If he bet this game, it would have been before we got to him. I know he's a capable quarterback, but he's also capable of screwing us over. The next game won't be so easy. We'll have to watch him closely."

"Well, he couldn't have played much better tonight," Mark concluded.

"True," Jack said as he headed for the door. "See you on the other side."

*

The gym was dimly lit and extensively decorated. All the students were decked out in dresses and suits. The band had yet to begin and soft music filled the void.

Jack surveyed the gym for Jenna and saw her surrounded by her friends. As he approached Jenna, several classmates greeted him. Trying hard to get to where Jenna stood, Jack tried desperately not to be rude to classmates who were congratulating him on the game.

Relieved at having made his way through the crowd, Jack greeted Jenna and her friends. He was careful to acknowledge each girl in the circle. At last, he came to his date.

"Congratulations. The crown fits you well," Jack remarked.

"Thanks, Jack" Jenna responded as she took two steps toward him, wrapping her arms around his neck.

Jack leaned in and kissed her on the cheek. The couple separated to include the others in their conversation.

"What were you girls discussing just now?" Jack asked.

"What do you think?" Victoria answered, mocking Jack.

"Perhaps you were discussing the time Jenna got clobbered with a dozen roses at a football game."

Gritting her teeth, Jenna stepped into Jack and punched him in the stomach.

"C'mon Jenna, I was just kidding."

Jack grabbed Jenna and pulled her in for another hug.

"Is there a master of ceremonies for this dance or what?" Victoria asked Jack.

"I think Student Council is handling that. Isn't that Bobby Carson, the Student Council President, up there on the stage?" Jenna asked, wondering how things were supposed to proceed.

"What's up with that guy's pants?" Victoria pointed out. "They don't match his jacket."

"They match," Jack said in Bobby's defense.

"No. They don't. Those pants are navy blue and his jacket is black," Victoria explained. "Are you color blind?"

"No, I think the light is throwing you."

"Will both of you just shut up about the pants?" Jenna shouted. "He's about to start."

Bobby picked up the microphone from its stand while the band took its place.

"Good evening ladies and gentlemen, seniors and underclassmen. It is my privilege and honor to introduce you to Sacred Heart's Homecoming Queen, Jenna Witherspoon."

Bobby motioned toward Jenna and everyone turned to look at her.

"Please come forward and take your place on the throne."

Jenna glided through the cheering crowd until she stood in front of her chair on the stage. She waved as the gathering of students continued to applaud her.

"Traditionally," Bobby continued, "the queen and her escort have the first dance, but this year, Jenna's escort, Jack Bowden, has asked if he could sing a song in her honor. So, here is Jack Bowden."

With the room completely darkened, two spotlights appeared on Jack and Jenna. Everyone was expecting Jack to serenade Jenna with an appropriate love song. Jack, instead, opened with the introduction to Queen's 'We are the Champions' which everyone recognized immediately. Jack moved in close with his electric guitar and with effortless movements filled the room with heart pounding chords. When he began to sing, everyone in the room joined in. The audience was singing so loud that Jack could barely hear himself. When he sang, "no time for losers", Jenna put the 'L' sign on her forehead and pointed at Jack. The crowd swayed back and forth, arm in arm as Jack brought the song to its conclusion.

When Jack finished the song, Jenna stood, placed her hands on each of Jack's cheeks, and kissed him under the spotlights.

"You really know how to work a crowd," Jenna complimented.

"Someone said I should sing at the homecoming dance," Jack reminded her.

"You should sing the flip side," Jenna suggested.

"Done," Jack responded and went right into 'We Will Rock You' to the crowd's delight.

Chapter 15

Jenna, her father, and the Nebraska State recruiter pulled into the driveway while Sam and Jack played catch in the front yard. When Jack saw the car, he walked over to greet them. He was happy to see Jenna so soon after their magical evening together and was anxious to hear what the recruiter had to say.

"Jack, this is Jim Tomer. He is from Nebraska State University," Mr. Witherspoon said, pointing to a very large man standing next to the passenger door.

Stepping forward, Jack offered his hand and said, "Nice to meet you, sir." Then, without hesitation, Jack introduced his brother and his parents who had come out the door when they heard the car pull into the driveway. "This is my brother, Sam and these are my parents, Walt and Clarice."

Mr. Tomer moved toward Sam and Jack's parents for customary handshakes and then turned back to face Jack. "Some game you had last night."

"Thank you, sir," Jack said, accepting the compliment.

"How would you rate Cumberland?" Mr. Tomer inquired.

"They weren't very good and I was playing really hard. You know, trying to impress you."

"Well, you did. You have good size and speed for a college prospect, but the hitting was most impressive. I've seen a lot of hits, but last night, it seemed to be one after another."

Jack blushed. He was proud, but he was also very humble. "Thank you. You are very kind."

Sam couldn't stand Jack's humility. "They don't call him 'The Hammer' for nothing."

"Sam!" Jack interrupted, "Please don't."

"No. I'm very interested," Mr. Tomer said, encouraging Sam's input.

"I could show you some hits that will make you squirm in your chair," Sam continued.

"How's that?" Mr. Tomer asked.

"I've been putting a little highlight video together for Jack. I have all of our games on video and I've been stringing Jack's best plays together. If you want, we can go inside and I'll show you?" Sam asked, looking for consensus.

"Sure, I'd love to see more," Mr. Tomer insisted.

The group made their way to the Bowden's basement and the seven of them sat in a semi-circle while Sam cued up the video.

"I'm going to set it to music, but right now it's still a little rough. The audio is at normal levels. It hasn't been amplified or anything. The speed is also at real time. There is no slow motion in the video," Sam explained.

Jenna stared at Jack and Jack returned the gaze. He knew he would be alone with her before the day was over. Jack could endure this delay for the prospect of playing for Nebraska

State. They both broke their visual connection and turned their attention to the screen.

Sam narrated the video. "This is Jack playing linebacker against Cranston West. He's going to blitz the weak side and sack the quarterback."

Just as Sam said, the haunting number fifty-one ran around the left side of the offensive line and blasted the Falcon quarterback, separating him from the ball. The camera followed Mark Johnson who picked the ball up and ran thirty-eight yards for the touchdown.

"The next play is a tackle Jack made on an East Greenwich running back going out of bounds," Sam continued.

The video clip showed Jack putting a murderous hit on the ball carrier and the collision sounded like a clap of thunder.

The group watching the screen all moved their heads back and grunted in response to the replay.

"I saw that one," Jenna recalled. "Remember Jack, I talked about that one in chemistry class."

"Yeah, I remember," Jack responded, thinking about how everyone listened intently as Jenna provided the details. "That was a good one."

Sam continued to describe each play while the group watched. With each play, Jack's father's pride began to show as he cheered plays he'd replayed in his head dozens of times. Mrs. Bowden was duly impressed by her youngest son's affection for his older brother. She was astonished that Sam would go to such lengths to provide Jack with such a gift.

The group watched in awe. Even Jack couldn't believe that he was this good. The video was remarkable and appeared like a professional production. The plays kept coming and they seemed to get better as the show went on.

Finally, Sam stopped the narration and addressed Jenna. "This next clip is the homecoming ceremony. Do you want to see it?"

Everyone turned toward Jenna anticipating her answer.

"Sure, what the heck? It's only you guys."

"Well, not exactly," Sam answered.

"What's that mean?" Jack asked, wanting an explanation.

"The network called. They said they were showing the piece on Sports Central tomorrow night as kind of a follow up to the story about us cheating."

"You gave them the video?" Jack shouted, trying hard not to lose his temper.

"No, of course not. They got the video from someone else. They called asking for comment, background information, that sort of stuff."

"What did you tell them?" Jack pressed.

"Nothing they didn't get from someone else. They just wanted to verify facts. I swear I didn't give them anything they didn't already know."

"Just play the video," Jenna cringed.

Both Sam and Jack stopped their conversation abruptly and Sam granted Jenna's wish.

After the video ended, everyone looked at Jenna for her reaction.

"What? It wasn't so bad," Jenna said, trying to lighten the mood.

"Wow! That was amazing!" Jack surmised.

Everyone turned to Jack.

"What was amazing? It was horrible," Mrs. Bowden interjected.

"No, it was amazing," Jack said again. "It was amazing how easily Jenna recovered. She's amazing, isn't she Mom?"

"Yes, she is," Mrs. Bowden answered, shifting her attention to Jenna.

Smiling, Jenna squeezed her dad's hand and said, "Thank you, Mrs. Bowden."

Turning the set off, Mr. Bowden asked Mr. Tomer rather bluntly, "Well, what do think? Does Jack have what it takes to play for Nebraska State?"

Pausing to consider his position, Mr. Tomer put his cards on the table. "I like you, Jack. I think you have it all. Nebraska State is prepared to offer you a full scholarship."

All eyes shifted to Jack. He looked at his family one by one. "That's great, Mr. Tomer. I'm truly appreciative of the offer, but I'm going to have to think about it."

"Think about it?" Jack's father asked. "What's there to think about?"

"Dad, please, it's not like I have to decide right now. Is it Mr. Tomer?" Jack asked, hoping for some time.

"No. It's normal for players to take some time to consider the commitment."

"When do I need to let you know?" Jack asked, wanting a timeline.

"The deadline for signing letters of intent is February 15th. I'd hope to know well in advance; let's say January 1st. I need to know where we stand in case you don't sign with us. We'll need to have a backup player ready at your position. You understand, right?"

"Sure. January 1st is very generous. Thank you," Jack said, expecting Mr. Tomer to make his way to the door. Instead, he wanted to speak to Sam about the Screaming Eagles' system for scouting other teams.

"So you're the brains behind the defense," Mr. Tomer charged.

"It's a team effort," Sam said humbly.

"This set up tells me different," Mr. Tomer observed, pointing to Sam's computer.

"How would you like to come to Nebraska State?" Mr. Tomer asked rather abruptly.

"Four years is a long time. Anything can happen between now and then," Sam said in a joking manner while he put his equipment away.

"I'm not talking four years. I'm talking next year, with Jack. You can work in the Athletic Department while you finish high school. I can fix it so you can live with Jack. What do you think about that?"

Sam saw that everyone's interest had peaked at this revelation.

Laughing, Sam said, "I hardly think that kind of decision is in my hands. Have you met my folks, Mr. and Mrs. Bowden?"

Chapter 16

Riding in the back of Mr. Tomer's Cadillac, Jack just smiled as he thought about his relationship with Jenna. With Jenna riding next to him, he thought about all the things he loved about her. He loved the softness of her skin, and the firmness of her muscles, the scent of her hair and the warmth of her touch. Jenna was not only great looking but she was great company, and what truly set her apart from other girls was that she liked football. Her affection for football turned Jack on more than anything. He'd never had a girlfriend that had a common interest as important as this one. Jack's enthusiasm heightened because at this very moment, they were pulling into the parking lot at the Nebraska State Football Stadium.

Jenna held Jack's hand and could easily tell what he was thinking, but didn't want to interrupt his happiness. She just put her head on his shoulder and closed her eyes, hoping they would spend many more evenings together like they had the night before.

Mr. Tomer looked at Jack in the rear view mirror, "You two are certainly quiet."

Sitting upright, Jenna and Jack smiled but did not speak.

"Are you thinking Nebraska State is where you want to be?" Mr. Tomer asked, as they drove closer to the stadium.

"Yes, sir," Jack responded. "There is nothing that would make me happier." Then, after a brief moment; Jack gave the opposing position. "Except that all my friends and family live in Rhode Island. I don't know how I'm going to be able to leave them."

"I understand," Mr. Tomer began. "It's a difficult choice to make. Try to think of it this way. It's only temporary. It's not like you're joining the Army. You can go back to Rhode Island during school breaks. Your friends will see you play on TV…nine Saturdays next fall, and I'm sure we'll go bowling, if you know what I mean."

"Oh, yes, I do," Jack answered then asked, "How many years will it be before you think I'll start."

"I expect the coach will want to red-shirt you this upcoming year. We have a senior All-American, John Wyman, coming back so we won't want to waste a year of your eligibility. After that, I expect you'll start for the next four years if you stay healthy."

"Wow! That's sooner than I had expected," Jack exclaimed looking at Jenna. "I thought I'd be sitting for three years."

"No. We wouldn't be recruiting you unless it was a mutually beneficial situation. We have plenty of walk-on players to fill the backup roles."

"Well, it certainly sounds good, but how will I know if I'm good enough? I don't want to make a fool of myself."

"Oh, you're good enough. I'm sure you feel a little insecure but your size already rivals that of our juniors and seniors. I expect you'll put on another thirty pounds after you start hitting the weight room a little more aggressively."

Jack imagined himself thirty pounds heavier looking down at his already oversized chest.

"I really haven't sat down with my folks yet, but it seems like my dad is all for it. I know my mom would miss me. I have to find out what she thinks before I can make any kind of commitment. There's also Jenna. We just started going out, but we've known each other for a while. I'd hate to leave you after things between us just got good," Jack added, turning his attention toward her.

Startled by this revelation, Jenna's eyes got really big. "Don't even start with that," she said to Jack, moving away from him so she could face him more directly. "This decision is about you. Don't concern yourself about other people. I've talked to everyone and they all want you to go. It's a matter of pride. To have one of their own on TV every Saturday and be able to sit in a bar, or dorm room, or even at home and say, 'That's Jack Bowden. I played with him at Sacred Heart.' It's almost as good as being there on the field with you. Everyone loves you, Jack. And everyone, including your mother, wants you to do what's best for you. Everyone wants you to go to Nebraska State . . . I even want you to go."

"Jenna, what about us?" Jack asked, becoming oblivious to the fact that Jenna's father was in the front seat.

"What about it? We've had a good time and we'll have more good times. It's not like we won't see each other again."

"It's not the same. I want to be with you."

Jenna got really serious and spoke very slowly to Jack. "It will disappoint me tremendously if you decide to stay in Rhode

Island because of me. I want you to go and I want you to be the best damn Nebraska State linebacker there ever was."

"Then will you come with me?" Jack asked, hoping for some consolation.

"I'll have to ask my dad," Jenna said, looking into the front seat.

Mr. Witherspoon didn't turn around. He only shook his head no.

"That means he'll think about it," Jenna said, knowing she could always get her way.

*

Sitting at midfield, the stadium and the crowd appeared much larger to Jack in real life than it did on TV. The crowd buzzed with excitement as the Nebraska State Mustangs led the Kansas Southern Bobcats late in the second quarter. The fans cheered every good play for the Mustangs and booed the Bobcats with every opportunity. Jack enjoyed the audience participation and at times got carried away, making much more noise than the surrounding fans.

During a timeout, Mr. Tomer and Mr. Witherspoon excused themselves to visit the concession stand, leaving Jack and Jenna alone. While Jack was pointing out various football rules that applied to the Mustangs current situation, a man in front of them burped out loud. He burped so loud, it drew the attention of everyone within earshot.

Jenna grabbed Jack's large soda and said, "Watch this." She gulped down about a third of it and moments later she expelled a great and hideous noise that Jack couldn't believe she was capable of.

The man sitting in front of them turned around to see who had dared to create a far more disgusting burp than his. Jenna laughed out loud when she caught the man's eye. The man, while still facing Jenna, proceeded to chug a healthy portion of his beer and let out an even louder belch and said, "Top that."

"Okay!" Jenna belted. She grabbed the man's beer out of his hand and chugged it. With drops of beer running down her chin and neck, Jenna stood on her seat and forced the air from her abdomen producing an ear splitting burp that made Jack back away from her in fear.

The entire section applauded the guiltless display and the fans closest to her crowded past Jack to give Jenna congratulatory high fives.

"Way to go, champ," Jack laughed as Jenna came down from her seat.

At this point, everyone in the area was chugging beer and seeing how loud they could burp. The chorus of burps inspired Jack to give it a go. He gulped down the rest of his soda and stood for all to hear. He let out an Earth shaking noise that quieted the crowd two aisles over. It was so loud that the players on the sidelines turned around to see the commotion.

Just then, Jenna's father and Mr. Tomer returned with two more sodas for Jack and Jenna. The group of burping strangers continued to belch in rhythm, but Jack and Jenna refrained as if they weren't a party to it.

After a few minutes, Mr. Witherspoon turned to his daughter and said, "What's going on here? This belching is most disturbing."

After a couple more minutes, Mr. Witherspoon stood and addressed the section. "Excuse me," he shouted, but no one paid him any attention. They just continued to burp away. "Excuse me," he yelled, attracting everyone's attention. "I did not come to this game to hear you people burp. I brought my daughter and her boyfriend here so they could enjoy themselves, not listen to your vile noise making."

The group of drunken people laughed hard when they recognized Jenna and Jack as the main instigators of the ruckus. Jenna and Jack tried to keep straight faces but snickered quietly when her father and Mr. Tomer looked the other way.

Then, with only two minutes left before halftime, the public address announcer came on the loudspeaker with regards to the halftime festivities. Three fans were to be selected to come onto the field and kick field goals for a chance to win a brand new car. When the announcer read the winning ticket numbers, Jack half-heartedly looked at his tickets and found that one of the two tickets he held matched the number called by the announcer.

Jack lost his breath and the blood ran from his head. He felt faint. He couldn't believe that from seventy thousand people, his was one of the three tickets selected.

"I won! I won!" he repeated louder and louder as he stood. "I won!" he yelled so that everyone around him could see.

"What did you win?" Jenna asked.

"I won a new car!" Jack exclaimed. "I wonder what kind of car it is. Who cares? I won it anyway."

"Let me see that ticket," Mr. Witherspoon said. "Yup, you won, but I'm afraid you didn't win the car, yet. You won an *opportunity* to win the car."

"What do you mean?" Jenna asked.

"You see, Jack has to make three field goals. He has to kick one from the twenty, then from the thirty, and finally, one from the forty yard line.

"What?" Jack sang as his mood dampened.

"C'mon, Jack. You can do it," Jenna encouraged.

Then the PA came on again and blared, "Would the three lucky winners come down to the field?"

Jack went straight down to the field and had to wait because the other winners were coming down from the second deck.

Only twelve rows separated Jack from Jenna. Jack waved to Jenna and shrugged his shoulders as if he didn't know what to do with himself. Waiting there made him nervous and he suddenly got hungry. Seeing Jenna eating peanuts made him even hungrier. Once he caught her attention, he motioned to his mouth that he wanted her to throw him a nut.

Jenna understood the gesture and threw a peanut. Jack took two steps to his left and caught the nut in his mouth. Unfortunately, Jenna didn't shell the nut and he had to spit it in his hand and remove the shell before eating it. Not wanting to dirty the field, he stuck the shell in his pocket. He chewed the nut and predictably wanted another one.

Seeing Jack putting the shell in his pocket in front of all the fans, Jenna decided to shell the next one for him. She threw it high and he caught it in his mouth without moving. The few fans watching, clapped with enthusiasm.

Jenna threw another one and when Jack caught it, more people than before applauded. Soon, Jack was caught up in a performance for literally thousands of spectators cheering with every nut. Jack had caught seven in a row when, all of sudden, he was on the spectra vision scoreboard. Seeing his image on the scoreboard inspired Jack to put one hundred percent effort into his nut catching. Then Jenna threw wildly and Jack had to take three steps to his right and dive for the nut. The nut hit him in the eye as he went headfirst into the ground, ruining his streak. The entire stadium was able to witness his final attempt and gave him a standing ovation.

Hamming it up, Jack waved to the camera, picked up the peanut and tossed it into the crowd.

After a short time, the other two contestants arrived down on the field with Jack. One was a plump woman in her thirties, and the other was a thin older gentleman in his sixties. Jack could easily see that these two individuals didn't have much chance of kicking one field goal, much less three.

The trio was led to the twenty yard line and each was given a tee and a football.

With the crowd cheering, the woman teed up the ball and backed away while looking up at the goal post thirty yards away. She ran straight up and swung her leg with all her might. She struck the ball near the top and the ball never left the ground. It dribbled down the field, bouncing right up to the goal line. A large gasp came from the crowd and the woman left the field not needing to take her other two kicks.

The older man lined up next. He, too, took a healthy gallop toward the ball and kicked the ball with all the force he could muster. His ball was airborne and had plenty of distance, but it sailed right and missed by three yards. He, also, retired to the sideline.

Next, it was Jack's turn. When the crowd saw Jack's size, it could sense he had a real opportunity to make some kicks. Jack placed the ball exactly between the hash marks and kicked it straight down the center of the field. The ball landed in the net and the cheers followed.

After the ball was returned, Jack set up on the thirty yard line. He had easily made kicks from the thirty in practice, and even though he wasn't the team's normal kicker, he always made a good percentage from this distance. He lined it up and kicked it through the uprights.

With two down and only one to go, Jack and the rest of the stadium felt like he might win the car. Just as he was lining the ball up on the forty, the stadium crew drove the car onto the field. It was a brand new cherry red Chevy Camaro.

Jack thought to himself what a coincidence it was that he was chosen out of seventy thousand people to kick field goals for a new car. He wondered what the probability was that they could have randomly selected a high school All-American to participate in this event. Not very likely, he concluded. Then, add to the fact that he owned an aging Pontiac Firebird. What were the chances of that? The car was bright red just like his, and just like the Nebraska State uniforms. This definitely added up to a fix in his mind.

This certainly was not the type of position he enjoyed being put in and he almost wanted to miss his last kick on purpose so he wouldn't feel like he was taking some kind of bribe. After all, if he suspected foul play, someone else would, too. With the crowd looking on and cheering in anticipation, Jack felt pressure to perform. Then he got an idea.

After Jack teed the ball up to kick the third field goal, he walked over to the man in charge of the event.

"Go ahead and kick the ball, son," the man said.

"Excuse me, sir," Jack shouted over the chorus of boos from the waiting crowd.

"Kick it," the man said, motioning toward the goal post.

"I will, but first I want you to do something for me," Jack asked.

"What? What is it?"

"I want you to announce that if I make the kick, I am donating the car to charity."

"You can do whatever you want with the car after you make the kick. Just kick the ball, will you?"

The crowd was beginning to get anxious and began voicing its disapproval about the delay.

"No. I'm not kicking that ball until the announcement is made over the PA system."

"Forget it, kid. If you don't kick the ball now, you lose it."

"Fine," Jack replied and began to walk off the field.

"Wait," the man said, have his bluff called.

After a three minute delay, the PA came on. "The field goal kicker has requested that we announce that he will donate the cash value of the car to charity if he makes this kick."

When the crowd heard this, they cheered in appreciation of Jack's good will.

Jack lined up the ball and came at it with great speed. He launched the football with incredible velocity. Unfortunately, the ball was a line drive knuckle ball. It twisted and turned in the frozen air. Jack couldn't tell if the ball had enough altitude from his perspective and bent over sideways, hoping the ball would make it above the crossbar. The ball struck the crossbar dead center and went straight up into the air almost to the top of the upright. It came straight down and hit the crossbar a second time before bouncing back and through the goal post.

The crowd went nuts.

Jack raised both fists in the air and walked off the field.

Chapter 17

When Jack returned to his seat, he was greeted with a hearty ovation. Jenna threw her arms around him, kissed him on the cheek and stood by proudly while her father addressed him.

"That was some good kicking," Mr. Witherspoon began. "One thing I don't understand. Why did you give it away? Don't you need a new car? I believe your car is getting pretty old."

Looking at Mr. Tomer, Jack didn't want to offend him with accusations. Instead, Jack took the high road. "I already have everything I need. Just being here is enough for me."

"Well, never the less, it was a good set of kicks, especially the last one," Mr. Witherspoon went on.

Mr. Tomer could see Jack was put off by the whole affair and chose to clear the air. "Boy, I sure am glad you donated that car before you made that kick. I'd have been in a heap of trouble. I was praying you would miss one of the first two kicks."

"What?" Jenna asked out of the depths of confusion.

"It was fixed. The contest was set up so I'd win the car. I thought Mr. Tomer was behind it but I guess that isn't the case."

"No, I wasn't. The people in the front office gave me these tickets and they knew I was bringing Jack. The rest I can only speculate as to what must have happened after that. I guess they didn't think Jack would be able to see through it, or they didn't think he would care."

"How did they know what kind of car I drive?" Jack asked Mr. Tomer.

"They don't have anything on their hands except time," Mr. Tomer explained. "I hope you're still considering playing for Nebraska State despite this little snafu."

"Oh, sure. I still want what's best for me. I just have to be smart about it."

The group proceeded to sit back and watch the Mustangs defeat the Bobcats in the second half.

*

The flight back to Rhode Island didn't land until after eleven and Jack didn't make it home until midnight. When he tip-toed into his room trying not to disturb his brother, he was amused to find that Sam had waited up for him.

"How was the game today?" Sam opened.

"You saw it, didn't you?" Jack asked, knowing he did.

"Yeah, I saw it. I also saw you," Sam revealed.

"Oh yeah," Jack answered in surprise. "What was I doing?"

"Well, let's see. The first time I saw you, you were kicking field goals for a brand new car you didn't seem to want. Then they showed you catching peanuts in your mouth. Then I got to see your highlights again on Sports Central."

"Sports Central? Huh? What's that? Three times this year."

"Yes, and we haven't even won the state championship yet," Sam chuckled.

"What did Dad say?" Jack wanted to know.

"He was pissed you gave away the car. Mom, however, thought you must have a good reason for doing what you did. What happened with the car, anyway?"

"It was supposed to be a random drawing to kick for the car, but it turned out that it wasn't. I put two and two together and decided I didn't want any part of it."

"What are you talking about?" Sam uttered, trying to figure out Jack's implication.

"Somebody was trying to entice me to go to Nebraska State. I might have lost my scholarship regardless of where I go to school."

"When did you figure it out?" Sam asked, trying to piece it together.

"When they brought out the car. It was a red Camaro."

"Wouldn't it be crazy if you were wrong and the whole thing was a coincidence?"

"Mr. Tomer came clean after the last kick and confirmed my suspicion," Jack told Sam as he climbed into bed.

"Now be quiet and don't say another word," Jack announced. "I'm going to sleep, right now."

"Good night," Sam responded, smiling in the dark.

*

The next evening, Jack invited the gang over for an impromptu party in honor of Jenna being on Sports Central. Sam had made a giant banner that hung across the basement wall. It read, 'Roses are red and Jenna is blue because she got blasted with flowers for beating you know who'.

After everyone arrived, Jenna quieted everyone and then said to the group, "Thank you all for coming tonight. It is my great honor to have you here to witness my very first time on television. I hope that you all are as grateful as I to have been part of this historic event."

Although the group was small, cheers went up and rang loudly in the small basement.

"Here, here," went Tim. "And thank you, Jenna, for being such a wonderful sport."

Again the group cheered Jenna's magnificent character.

Jenna picked up a spoon and struck it lightly against her glass to gain everyone's attention. "I have some news that you all will be very interested in." Knowing Jack's modesty, she correctly presumed Jack hadn't told anyone yet of his scholarship offer. "Jack has been offered a full ride to Nebraska State."

Cheers rang even louder as the grouped hollered in celebration.

"Wait, there's more," Jenna continued. "Sam was also offered a position."

Ken and Tim looked at Sam in amazement.

Reading their bewilderment, Sam mitigated their presumption. "Not playing football, scouting. You know . . . doing what I do best."

"Congratulations," Mark and Tim said together.

Holding everyone's attention Mark asked Jack, "Did you accept?"

"I'm thinking about it," Jack replied, looking at the floor.

"What's there to think about? It's Nebraska State," Mark sang as if nothing could be better.

"I know. I have a lot to consider. That's all."

Just as Mark and Ken were about to give Jack a rash for not jumping at the offer, Sam diverted their attention. "It's on!"

"Turn it up," Victoria yelled over the music.

"Well, if you didn't know how many petals were in a dozen roses, you know now," the commentator said as the show froze the video of the roses immediately after they struck Jenna in the face. "I counted 103, but if you look right there," the commentator paused, circling a small section of the screen with a white circle, "I can't tell if that is a whole bud or a single petal. We'll try to clean that up and have an answer for you tomorrow."

"So," a second commentator began, "Jack Bowden, who was featured on the show six weeks ago with his brother, is back in the news. With this unprecedented assault on the Sacred Heart Homecoming Queen by a losing candidate, it turns out that Jack Bowden, a shoe-in for All American, was dating Wendy Thompson, the girl holding the stems. They broke up only a week ago and Jack is now dating . . . you guessed it, Jenna Witherspoon, the girl who got clobbered."

"So it's not just about the crown. This fight is over the boy," the first one concluded.

"It gets better," the second one answered back. "Watch Jack come between the two girls and execute a classic fireman's carry. He picks up Wendy Thompson cleanly and carries her off the field."

"What I would have given to be at that game. Oh yeah, and there was a game. Sacred Heart scored an easy 56-0 victory and ran their state's best record to 9-0. Bowden made twenty tackles and then played guitar at the homecoming dance. That guy can do it all," the analyst said, finishing the story.

Jenna grabbed the remote and turned off the TV as soon as it was evident the show was going to commercial.

"I win homecoming queen, get assaulted, and the story ends up being about how great a football player you are," Jenna said to Jack with a tinge of sarcasm.

"I know. This kind of thing always seems to happen," Sam pointed out. "Remember? . . . "

"Shut it, Sam!" Jack interrupted before he could go into the details of the earlier story.

"No. This isn't right," Jenna insisted. "You need to make it right."

"What am I supposed to do?" Jack asked, seeking guidance.

"Compensation," Jenna answered, moving her eye brows up and down in a romantic motion.

Seeing Jenna's playful tactic, Victoria took control and said, "I think Jenna and Jack need some alone time. It's time for us to move this party to my house."

No one responded to Victoria's gentle nudge to get everyone out so she took a different tactic.

"Okay, everyone out!" she screamed.

This time everyone complied leaving Jack and Jenna alone for the evening.

*

The week of school passed quickly and Sacred Heart's playoff game was quickly approaching. Their opponent, the LaSalle Rams, finished the season 7-2 but endured a difficult schedule. Their only losses came to East Providence and Toll Gate. Jack and Sam had worked diligently to prepare for the Rams. They knew the Rams would change up the offense and prove to be worthy opponents. With several game films of the

Rams, Sam was able to put together a solid game plan to cover their featured players.

Both the offense and defense worked in harmony during the week of practice. Chuck seemed to be in line. His passing was certainly in tune and he carried a positive attitude throughout the week. He even encouraged the defense when they made outstanding plays. Jack and the defense appeared convinced that Chuck would give a credible effort.

At game time, the Screaming Eagles were healthy. Ken's thigh had healed nicely and with the exception of Matt Wilks absence at defensive end, all other positions were filled and ready to go.

Coach Dawson had given final instructions and the Screaming Eagles took the field looking for their first championship bid in five years.

The Screaming Eagles received the ball on the opening kick and started their first drive from their own twenty-nine. With the wind blowing squarely in their faces, Coach Dawson used a variety of running plays to combat the elements. First, he ran Cruise on an option left, then Singleton up the middle. He used Tanner on a reverse and then Singleton to the left. The Screaming Eagles were making good progress, chewing up yardage and the clock at the same time.

The momentum appeared to be on Sacred Heart's side when Cruise was tackled on an option play. When everyone returned to the huddle, Cruise lay on the field, moaning like he'd been in a car accident. When the trainer tried to assist him off the field, he collapsed. He didn't move again until he was taken away on a stretcher. It became apparent to Coach Dawson and everyone else in the stadium that Chuck wouldn't return.

While the teams waited for the ambulance to arrive, Coach Dawson approached Sam. "I guess you're in. We won't pass while we are going against the wind. Just take your time and make sure you don't fumble. We can win this game on defense. As long as we don't make any mistakes on offense, we'll be fine. Any questions?"

"No, sir," Sam answered with a lump in his throat.

"Good. Now get in there and take a few practice snaps. Tell Huntington to just hand you the ball. Don't let him jerk you around. Got it?"

"Yes, sir," Sam said, running onto the field.

The home crowd was accustomed to seeing Sam play defense and everyone cheered his entrance into the game. The Rams, however, had never seen a smaller quarterback and began salivating at the opportunity to spoil Sam's debut.

It was second and ten at the Rams' thirty-four. Sam called Singleton for a dive and broke the huddle. When Sam looked up at the Rams' defense, he grew nervous when he saw their intense expressions. When he took the ball from center, the ball slipped through his hands and bounced awkwardly when it hit the ground. The Rams recovered and the Screaming Eagles lost a valuable scoring opportunity.

Sam remained on the field to play defense as the units shuffled on and off the field. With his head hung low, Sam felt an arm come around his shoulder pads. When he looked up, he saw his big brother looking down at him.

"It's okay, Sam. The Hammer and his friends are on the field now. We'll get that one back. By the time you're through today, you're going to be the hero that got us to the state championship."

Sam smiled and shook his head walking into the huddle.

"Listen to Sam for the call. Key on your man and watch for the double team," Jack ordered.

When the Rams came to the line, Sam and the rest of the defense recognized the formation and could easily predict the play. The defense moved to the spot and stopped the Ram runner cold. Jack and Sam could hardly believe that the Rams didn't make any adjustments to their offense.

The Screaming Eagles' defense dominated the first series and the Rams punted. With the ball on the twenty-five and still heading into the wind, Coach Dawson called for a series of running plays. Singleton to the left, Singleton to the right, and Singleton up the middle. Singleton moved the ball at a steady clip behind his big front line. But as the series continued, the Ram defenders began to anticipate Singleton's runs and the gains became less and less. It became evident to Coach Dawson that this one dimensional offense could not survive the day.

With a third and two on the Rams' forty-eight, Coach Dawson called for a slant pattern to Tanner over the middle. Just as Sam was rearing to throw his first pass, he was sacked for a six yard loss. The Screaming Eagles were forced to punt and the defense came back onto the field.

"What was that?" Jack asked Sam when he met him on the field.

"What?" Sam asked defensively.

"Did that guy come through unblocked or were you in slow motion?" Jack queried.

"It was only a two step drop. He hit me before I even took the second step back."

"Who missed their block then?" Jack continued.

"Who do you think?" Sam answered with his hands on his hips.

"Hamilton?"

"You got it."

*

The second quarter began with the Screaming Eagles taking possession on their own forty-two in a 0-0 tie. Now playing with the wind, Coach Dawson decided to open up the passing game. He called for a post to Shaffer, but when Sam dropped back, he was sacked. Again, it was Hamilton's man that came unabated.

Dusting the cold dirt from his body, Sam's hands stung from the fall. He approached Hamilton who was nearly twice his size and confronted him.

"Look, if you're not going to block, get the hell off the field!"

Hamilton retaliated to the insult and pushed Sam in the chest, sending him to the turf. He pointed his finger down at Sam and said, "Shut up, runt!"

With Sam and Hamilton at odds, the offense was in shock when the play came in.

"Out and up to Tanner," Sam called. "On two."

When the ball was hiked, Hamilton's man easily broke free and despite Sam's attempt to elude him, he was sacked for a second consecutive play.

With third and twenty from their own thirty-two, Sam just turned his back on the offensive line and stood facing the ground, wondering what to do.

All the while, Jack knew full well what to do. Without conferring with Coach Dawson, he strapped on his helmet and ran onto the field. When he arrived at the huddle, he jerked Hamilton out.

"You're out, Hamilton."

"What the . . . ?" Hamilton objected.

"Coach says you're out. I'm in, now get out of here."

"Screw you, Bowden!" Hamilton barked, stripping his helmet from his head then throwing it to the ground as he retreated to the sideline. He kicked his helmet toward the bench, lumbering off the field.

"Thanks, Jack," Sam smiled. "Did the coach send in a play?"

"Yeah," Jack fibbed. "He said to run the left side screen to Matt."

"On one," Sam ordered then broke the huddle.

When Sam took the snap, he rolled to the right and looked up the field at Tanner and Shaffer leading the safeties away from the intended receiver. He then turned and threw the ball to Matt in the left flat. Playing left tackle, Jack released as soon as he saw the ball leave Sam's hand. Leading Matt down the left sideline, Jack threw two bone crushing blocks while Matt darted in and out of tacklers on his way to a seventy yard touchdown catch and run.

When Jack picked Matt up in the end zone as part of the scoring celebration, Matt looked at him as if he were a stranger.

"Oh come on, Matt," Jack said, slapping his back. "It was a hell of a play. Give me some skin."

Matt slapped Jack's hand and jogged off the field now wishing he'd been part of Jack's defense all year.

The defense went right back to work. On first down, Mark blitzed a play action pass and sacked the Rams' quarterback for an eight yard loss. On second down, Sam doubled the wide receiver and deflected the pass out of bounds. On third and eighteen, Jack came through the line on a stunt and caused the quarterback to fumble as he went down. Ken pounced on the loose ball and the Screaming Eagles' offense was given a short field.

Now brimming with confidence because Jack was playing left tackle, Sam had a spring in his step. Looking over the field, Sam hit Tanner on a crossing route for twelve yards, then Shaffer on a slant for seven more. Then with his receivers were covered, he turned a roll out pass play into a run for six more yards. On first and goal, Sam handed the ball to Singleton on a draw and the big tailback galloped into the end zone untouched. The Screaming Eagles led 14-0.

The Screaming Eagles parlayed their first half momentum into a 35-7 rout. LaSalle did manage a lone touchdown on a kick return, but Sacred Heart dominated on both offense and defense. Just as Jack had said, Sam became a hero. He didn't score any touchdowns or make any Earth shattering plays, but he played a solid game at quarterback and he proved that they didn't need Cruise to win.

There was no celebration after the game. It was business as usual. The Screaming Eagles had not yet reached their goal of a state championship and winning this game was just the next step to that end. The players walked off the field more serious about their quest for a championship than ever before.

Chapter 18

"Did you bring it?" Tim asked Jack as Tim drove his mom's minivan into Jenna's driveway.

"Yeah, I brought it," Jack answered. "This is going to be so lame. Of all the stupid ideas, this is the stupidest."

"Honk the horn. I don't want to get out," Jack directed. "I'll be in there forever talking to Jenna's dad."

Tim obliged and honked the horn twice.

The boys continued to wait for the tardy girls. Jack checked his watch and it was a quarter after seven. They were supposed to meet Ken and Mark at seven thirty and Jack easily deduced they wouldn't make it.

"Ten and zero, I can't believe it. It all seemed so easy," Jack said, referring to their perfect season.

"It's supposed to be easy when you have the country's best middle linebacker on defense. I think the defense only gave up four touchdowns all season," Tim said, not giving it much thought.

"One more to go," Jack muttered, thinking about their championship game with East Providence on Saturday.

"Have you heard anything about Chuck?" Tim asked, trying to pass the time.

"No. I haven't. We should check on him. It's the right thing to do," Jack replied.

"He's such a jerk. I can't imagine anyone checking on him without a gun to their head," Tim countered, feeling no obligation. "It's a good thing Sam was able to take over for him. If it were Walters, I don't know if we would have won last night."

"That's right," Jack agreed, turning around to acknowledge his brother's achievement.

"Thanks," Sam said, showing genuine gratitude for their remarks. "How about Hamilton? He's the real jerk. I swear he was missing those blocks on purpose."

"I heard he quit," Tim jumped in. "When the coach told him he was sitting next week, he threw a tantrum and quit."

"I guess that means I'm playing both ways next week," Jack assumed.

"If Chuck isn't any better, I will be as well," Sam added.

The door to Jenna's house flew open and Jenna, Victoria, and Sarah skidded down the driveway to Tim's van. When Sam opened the door, he moved to the rear seat and was joined by Sarah.

Driving down the winding streets back to his own house, Tim could see Sarah and Sam kissing in the rear view mirror.

"Hey, break it up back there!" Tim shouted to everyone's surprise.

Jack turned around from the front seat to see what Tim was talking about and saw his brother blush with embarrassment.

"Quarterbacks!" Jack smiled. "They always get the girls."

Pausing, Sam retorted. "The good ones do."

Tim pulled in his driveway and found Ken, Mark, Moriah, and Hannah waiting for them.

The house was fully decorated for Christmas. Tim's parents went all out. Lights lined the shrubs and the house. A wreath was mounted on the door and in each window. A twelve foot Christmas tree sat in the corner of the living room and was surrounded by beautifully wrapped presents. The mantle above the fireplace was trimmed with ornaments and three stockings hung above the fireplace.

Christmas music was playing softly when the teenagers entered the main room. Tim took everyone's coats and threw them in the closet, not wanting to take time to hang them up.

"Eggnog, anyone?" Tim asked upon his return to the living room.

"Sure," Jenna and Hannah answered for everyone.

Five minutes later, Tim brought in a tray full of drinks.

"This is nice, Tim. It's really generous of your parents to let us have our party here," Victoria said, looking at the lavish décor. "My parents would never trust you guys not to destroy our house."

"They're okay, I guess. I should buy them presents this year."

"What are you doing?" Jenna asked Jack while he sat on the sofa.

"Nothing," Jack answered without concern.

"Yes, you are. What is up with your eyebrow?"

"Nothing," Jack answered again, pulling on one of his eyebrows.

"You've been pulling that eyebrow since we got here. Let me see that," Jenna ordered, climbing on top of him to look at the hair that perched above his eye.

"Jesus!" Jenna exclaimed, examining it.

"What is it?" Victoria asked from across the room.

"Get over here, Vic. Look at this," Jenna urged.

"Oh my God! Look at that!" Victoria shouted as she joined Jenna hovering over Jack's eyebrow.

"Stop it!" Jack ordered, tossing both girls aside.

"What is it?" Moriah asked with peaked curiosity.

"It's Jack's eyebrow. One of the hairs has mutated and is about two inches long," Victoria explained.

"It is not," Jack refuted, putting his hand over his eyebrow so no one could see. "I must have missed it when I was trimming them."

"You trim your eyebrows?" Mark asked in surprise. "That's like a girl thing, isn't it?"

"If he didn't, it would be one large unibrow." Sam offered.

"Oh, yeah," Jack countered to his little brother. "You want to open up your closet of freaky habits."

"No," Sam replied, thinking of all the things Jack could say about him.

"Then shut it," Jack ordered.

Looking at his watch, Ken said, "If we wait any longer, we won't make it."

"Holy cow! It's almost nine o'clock," Jack announced. "They'll be in bed in less than an hour. If we don't go now, we can't go at all."

"What are you guys talking about?" Jenna asked amongst all the confused girls.

"We have to leave now," Jack announced, standing up.

"But I don't want to leave now," Sarah objected. "This is so romantic."

"Where are we going?" Victoria asked Tim.

"It's a surprise. You'll know when we get there."

Tim hustled to the closet, picked up the heap of coats and passed them out one by one.

The ten teenagers all crammed themselves into Tim's minivan and took off.

"Great, it's starting to snow again," Tim complained.

"It'll only make it better," Jack encouraged.

Tim pulled into a driveway of a ranch house that no one recognized.

"Where are we?" Jenna asked, becoming alarmed.

"Ms. Thomas' house," Sam answered, trying to calm her down.

"Ms. Thomas, Jack's English teacher, Ms. Thomas?" Jenna asked in disbelief. "What are we doing here?"

"It's called pandering for grades," Mark interjected, unenthused about the endeavor.

Pulling his guitar out of the rear hatch, Jack altered the perception. "We're singing Christmas carols."

"Christmas carols?" Jenna asked as if she didn't hear Jack correctly.

"Yup, Christmas carols," Jack confirmed.

"Mark, Sam, and Ken, you build the snowman right here. Sarah, Hannah, and Moriah, you three lay down right there and make snow angels. Vicki, Jack, Jenna and I will stand here. What song are we singing, Jack?" Tim asked for everyone.

"You guys know 'Jingle Bells'?"

"Yeah, I think we can handle that," Tim choked. "What else?"

"How about 'Santa's Coming to Town' and 'Come All Ye Faithful'. Three songs should be enough if we want to make it to Mr. Stamps' and Mr. Cain's before ten o'clock."

"Ring the doorbell," Tim said to Jenna.

"You ring the doorbell." Jenna countered.

"No, you ring the doorbell," Tim said again.

"Jack, you ring the doorbell," Jenna said to Jack, hoping he would remove her unwanted responsibility.

"I can't. I'm holding the guitar."

"Okay," Jenna finally agreed and walked up to the front porch and rang the doorbell.

The front porch light came on and just as Jenna was backing down the steps to join the rest of the group, all five boys took off running and hid behind the van. Just as Victoria was about to scream at them, the front door swung open and there stood Ms. Thomas with her husband and their three kids.

They stared down the stairs at the five girls waiting for a reason as to why they rang the doorbell. With Sara, Moriah, and Hannah covered in snow from making snow angels, the girls looked at each other and the Thomas' without knowing what to do next.

After ten seconds that seemed like ten years, Jenna started to sing the words to 'Jingle Bells' and the other girls joined in. After they finished the first verse, the boys came out from behind the van and Jack began to play along. When the boys walked up to join their girlfriends, they also sang along with the music.

Ms. Thomas recognized the group right away and pointed out who they were to her three children. Her son, who was ten, recognized Jack from the football team and waved excitedly to get his attention. When the group was done with the three songs, Ms. Thomas thanked them and wished them well. Her family returned inside with smiles on their faces.

The five girls were not as happy and needed to exact revenge upon their boyfriends for their cruel act of abandonment. As soon as the front door closed, the girls began yelling and punching their male counterparts. The melee turned into a giant snowball fight. The boys gave up in good spirits and let the girls pummel them so they would be able to make up.

After their reconciliation, the group headed out to their other teachers houses and repeated their performance without any more practical jokes.

*

Later that same evening, Jenna and Jack broke free from the group and headed for Tim's pool house.

Jack and Jenna cuddled in the dark on the sofa.

"Jack," Jenna began.

"Yes," Jack answered.

"When are you going to teach me to drive a stick shift?"

"Not now, I can assure you."

"Oh c'mon, I'm not a bad driver," Jenna said playfully, punching Jack in the stomach.

Pausing between kisses, Jenna envisioned their future. "Did you get your letter of intent from Nebraska State yet?"

"Yeah, I got it today," Jack replied, looking up at the ceiling.

"Did you sign it?"

"Not yet. Coach Dawson wants to have a press conference."

"Guess what?" Jenna asked, propping herself up so she could see Jack's face.

"What?" Jack played along.

"I got a scholarship offer to play tennis," Jenna announced proudly.

"That's great!" Jack congratulated. "I didn't know you were that good."

"Me either," Jenna responded as she stood up on the sofa.

"What school gave you that offer?" Jack asked.

"Nebraska State University!" Jenna shouted as she began jumping up and down making Jack bounce on the cushion.

"Stop it, you're going to hurt me," Jack begged right before Jenna lost her balance and fell on top of him.

Jenna was so light, he barely felt her weight come crashing down on his midsection.

"Wait a minute," Jack posed. "This is very suspicious. Don't you think you got the scholarship to entice me to sign with them?"

"Duh," Jenna replied. "Apparently, if you date a football prospect, and it might enhance his chances of going to Nebraska State, they might offer the girlfriend something to create more incentive. It just so happens, I play tennis."

"And you're okay with that?" Jack asked.

"Sure," Jenna giggled.

"Just how good a tennis player are you?" Jack wanted to know.

"I can beat your butt," Jenna bragged, spanking Jack on the rear.

Chapter 19

With only five days before their championship game against the East Providence Townies, the Screaming Eagles were determined to fine tune their game plan and make every play flawless in hopes of completing their perfect season. The offense and defense finally came together. With Jack and Sam playing both ways, there was no infighting. With Cruise and Hamilton gone, the other offensive players were able to focus on the game, rather than the rivalry.

The offensive players supported Sam and made every effort to complete their assignments and execute their blocks. The receivers were diving for passes, the backs were running hard and the linemen were blocking everything that moved.

The defensive players were also supportive. During practice, they played as hard as they could, trying to give Sam the look and feel for the competition he would face the following Saturday. The defense came with fierce pass rushes and disguised its coverage to give the freshman quarterback a formidable test.

After Monday's practice the players were all upbeat when they left the field. The players' uniforms were stained with grass, blood and dirt, but their spirits were high. They knew they had given maximum effort and were playing with championship intensity.

Once in the locker room, the players were discussing game strategy as they changed. All at once, the locker room fell silent when Chuck Cruise and Coach Dawson emerged from the coach's office.

With his arm around Cruise, Coach Dawson made an announcement to the attentive team. "Chuck is okay. He'll be at practice tomorrow and he'll be our quarterback on Saturday."

Cruise smiled weakly and left the room before anyone had a chance to question the nature of his injury.

After the coach had returned to his office, the stunned players speculated on Chuck's return.

"That's just great!" Ken remarked in sarcasm. "Choke is back."

"What was his injury again?" Tim asked aloud. "Didn't he have an ingrown hair or something?"

"Yeah, up his butt," Mark joked, joining the folly.

"This is wrong," Jack said seriously. "This can't be happening."

Dejected, Sam sat on the locker room bench with nothing to say.

"We have to do something," Mark said, rallying his friends. "Cruise is going to screw us. We have to go to the coach and tell him about Chuck's gambling."

"With what?" Jack asked. "We don't have any evidence. We can't prove anything. We'll just end up looking like idiots."

The five players sat in a row with their heads in their hands trying to imagine how to get Chuck out of Saturday's game.

Surprisingly, Matt Singleton walked up to them and said, "I'll do it."

The bewildered boys looked up at Matt.

"What?" Tim asked, not knowing what he had said.

"I'll do it. I can prove Chuck's been gambling," Matt assured them.

"How?" Tim asked in disbelief.

"Leave it to me. It'll be done tomorrow."

"Why?" Jack muttered.

"Because it's the right thing to do."

Jack put his hand on Matt's shoulder and nodded in agreement.

*

The next day, Matt showed up at lunch and sat down with the group of boys he'd known for a dozen years, but with which he rarely interacted.

"I got it," Matt announced, hoping his evidence would not only keep Chuck out of Saturday's game, but more importantly, help him join the group he'd wanted for friends for the past three months.

"What did you get?" Mark asked skeptically.

"You'll see," Matt responded, putting a tape recorder on the table. "The voices are Chuck's bookie, Steve Walton, and me."

"You wore a wire?" Tim laughed. "This is unbelievable!"

"Listen to the tape," Matt directed.

The boys sat patiently while the tape spun in the recorder.

"I can't hear anything," Ken whined.

"Give it a minute," Matt barked. "I had to turn it on before I approached him."

211

The taped conversation began shortly thereafter.

"Hey, how's it going?"

"Okay. What's up?"

"Chuck said I might be able get some action with you."

"Chuck said that, huh?"

"Yeah."

"Whatever. Who do you want?"

"What's the line on our game, Saturday?"

"You're favored by two, but you don't want to bet that game?"

"Why not?"

"Cause there's a good chance you'll lose."

"I don't think so. I am quite positive we'll win."

"No, you won't."

"Did Chuck bet our game?"

"No. I wouldn't let him."

"Why not?"

"After last week's fiasco, he owes me big."

"What happened last week?"

"You guys were favored by two touchdowns. Chuck figured if he got hurt, there was no way you'd win by that much. Who would've figure that punk Bowden would come in and have the game of his life? Cruise's miscalculations cost me three G's. So I told him if he throws Saturday's game, I'd let him live."

Silence followed on the tape for a few uncomfortable seconds.

"So who do you want?" the bookie asked for the second time.

"Forget it. I just wanted to bet on our game."

"Hey. If you tell someone or do something to screw this up, your pal Cruise is going to get it. You got that."

"Yeah, I got it."

Then the tape went silent.

The boys all looked up from the tape recorder and stared at each other in shock.

"What do we do now?" Ken asked Jack.

"I think we should go to the coach with it," Tim suggested.

"No. I don't think so. If we take it to the coach, it might get out and we might end up forfeiting all of our games. We should definitely keep this between us. Let's go have a little talk with Chuck."

The group of boys could see Chuck two tables over talking with Sue and they all swarmed over to his table. Sue felt the seriousness of the mood and left before the exchange commenced.

After the boys sat down, Jack spoke for the group. "So, you couldn't do it, could you?"

"Do what?" Chuck answered, looking at Matt for help.

"Leave well enough alone. You kept right on gambling. That stunt you pulled last week, getting injured on the first drive didn't sell. You're still mixed up in it and we're not going to let you play Saturday."

"I have to play," Chuck said, shaking. "They'll kill me if I don't."

"No, you won't play and here's why. If you step one foot on that field this week, we'll go to Coach Dawson with some evidence that we've acquired from a guy you may know, Steve Walton. If the coach gets this, not only will you not play, but your chances for a scholarship will be history. Our team will hate you for the rest of your life as will the entire student body."

"But if I don't play, they'll break both of my kneecaps," Chuck whispered, trembling from fear.

"You'll just have to come up with a real injury that is a little more convincing than last week's."

"What are you going to do, break my arm?" Chuck asked, sticking his throwing arm out on the table.

"No. We'll leave this one up to you. You'll only have until tomorrow, and don't even think of showing up for practice today."

*

Practice rolled around that afternoon and the boys were waiting to see if Chuck would adhere to Jack's warning. Chuck was a no show and the later practice continued without him, the more relieved the boys felt. With only twenty minutes left, they were convinced their intervention had been successful.

After the boys had returned to the locker room, Coach Dawson came out of his office and stood before the team.

"I have some bad news. Chuck's grandmother in Arizona has passed away and he will be in Phoenix for the funeral on Saturday.

Jack and his friends snuck looks of skepticism toward each other but accepted the coach's announcement.

Then, after pausing for the news to sink in, Coach Dawson looked at Sam. "You're back in. Get ready."

Sam nodded and the team went back to its business.

*

The next three days sailed by. Chuck didn't show up at school and no one had seen him around town. Now that he was through for the year, Jack and his friends could stop worrying about Chuck and his problems.

It turned out that Chuck's grandmother hadn't died. He had made that part up to save face with Coach Dawson. He did, in fact, go to Phoenix that week. Apparently, Chuck moved to Arizona out of fear. He figured moving two time zones away was less painful than two broken legs. The boys learned of his move when his record request leaked out of the guidance office.

Practices were running smoothly and the hype before the big game continued to grow. Students and teachers were patting players on the back and wishing them luck. Pep squad members were leaving notes and candy in their lockers. The cheerleaders hung large banners around school with phrases of encouragement.

On Friday, the school held a pep rally in the gym to honor the team. The players wore their jerseys and the cheerleaders and the band were dressed in their uniforms as well. While the band played, the students filed into the gym for the ceremony. The players waited in the locker room for the rally to begin.

Sam sat silently running his hands through his short brown hair.

"What's going to happen up there?" Sam asked Jack who sat nearby.

"They just want a chance to honor the team. Make everyone feel good about our success. This time next week, we'll be on Christmas break and when we get back, it'll all be over. No one but us will care whether we won or lost. It'll seem like it didn't even happen," Jack predicted.

"Yeah, I know that, but what's actually going to happen upstairs?"

"They'll call your name and you'll step forward and wave and then you'll step back. That's about it."

"That's it?"

"Yup, that's it."

Then a voice called down to the locker room. "They're ready. Come on out."

One by one, the boys walked through the door that led to the gymnasium. When the first player reached the entrance, the audience reacted with a heart stopping applause. The band kicked in and the players slowly jogged out to center court and made a line that stretched the length of the floor.

Father Joseph, the school's principal, welcomed the boys and congratulated them on their season before turning the microphone over to Coach Dawson. Coach Dawson went into a lengthy speech about how hard the team had worked to this point and how appreciative he was for the student body's support. The speech grew to such length that Mark and Tim began to yawn dramatically behind Coach Dawson, drawing laughter from the crowd.

At last, Coach Dawson began the introductions. He stated each player's name, year and position. Each player stepped forward just like Jack had said and received a gratuitous applause and returned to their place in line. After all the players had their turn, Coach Dawson asked Jack to say a few words.

Before Jack could utter a word, the crowd stood and applauded their star linebacker. When the noise level subsided, Jack began his impromptu speech.

"I'd like to thank you all for being such loyal and spirited fans."

Applause rang through the gym before the echo from the microphone faded. Jack took a step back after being surprised by the overwhelming response. The crowd continued to cheer him and every time he stepped forward to continue, the crowd's noise swelled to delay him. He ultimately had to wave the crowd down so he could resume. The student body complied and allowed Jack to finish.

"We'd also like to thank Coach Dawson for his leadership."

Again the student body erupted with noise and rose to offer Coach Dawson their support. Jack had to calm the students again, but thankfully, it was not as difficult as before.

Motioning to the line of teammates behind him, he continued, "We'd like to invite you all to our final game of the season for the Division I State Championship against East Providence tomorrow."

The students cheered louder than ever and the players all lifted their fists in the air. They began giving each other high fives and raising their index fingers to indicate their number one status.

After a five minute celebration of their impending championship bid, Jack waved the crowd down once again. Two cheerleaders then brought out an enormous three foot high trophy and handed it to Jack. Jack cradled the trophy against his hip with his left hand and held the microphone with his right. "Finally, I'd like to present the Most Valuable Player Award for this season. The football team took a vote and this player clearly brought this team to a level we couldn't have expected. He worked harder than anyone and played well beyond any expectations. Everyone looks up to him . . . figuratively. This year's most valuable player is my little brother, Sam Bowden."

Jack turned to face Sam amongst the deafening roar that filled the gym. As Sam approached Jack, Jack set the trophy on the floor and embraced his brother. Tears welled up in Sam's eyes as he accepted the trophy. Jack lifted Sam's hand in the air amidst the noise. Sam then turned to face his teammates. He squarely looked at Ken, Tim, and Mark and nodded in appreciation to each.

Chapter 20

Both Jack and Sam went to bed early, but neither could sleep. Both boys lay motionless, looking out the window into the night.

"Jack," Sam said from the top bunk.

"Yeah," Jack willfully responded.

"Are you going to Nebraska State next year?"

"Yeah, I think so. I'm going to miss home, but I think I need to move on."

"It'll be weird around here without you," Sam said, wishing he would stay.

"I know. It'll be weird not being here. I guess this means you're not accepting Mr. Tomer's offer to come with me," Jack joked.

"Are you kidding? I've got my glory days ahead. I'm the starting quarterback for the best team in the state and I've got a girlfriend that is way out of my league. Things couldn't be better. Plus, with you gone, Mom and Dad will give me whatever I want."

"Sounds good. I hope you enjoy it," Jack said in all sincerity.

Then Sam stopped thinking about himself and considered Jack.

"Damn. Tomorrow is your last game, isn't it?"

"Yeah," Jack said getting all choked up. With tears running out of his eyes in the dark, he could hardly talk without letting his brother know he was crying. Holding it back the best he could, Jack explained the feeling, "I suppose it's like graduation. Remember when you left middle school . . . all the memories you had? You can never get it back. The building and the teachers are still there, but you don't belong anymore. It's a weird feeling."

"It's not like you're dying or anything," Sam said, trying to lighten the mood.

Jack didn't answer. He just laid there.

Sam moved his head to the side of the bunk to see Jack's face. He had an expression of angst. He wasn't happy for it to be over. Why would he be? He was the best there was and after tomorrow, it would be nothing but a memory. He wouldn't play anymore, at least not here.

"I forgot to thank you for the MVP award. It was great to win, but I know you. You made it happen for me." Sam said, expressing gratitude. "Today was the best day of my life."

"You're welcome," Jack answered. "You deserved it. Without your scouting and play calling, we could never have achieved as much as we have. The quarterbacking put it over the top."

"Don't you think it's amazing how our opponents didn't really attempt to change their offensive schemes after our system was reported in the news? Even after it went public, we just rolled over almost every team we faced."

Jack thought for a minute and then offered a simple analysis. "This is high school. Those coaches have been using those same plays and formations for twenty years. On top of that, if they did try to change everything in midseason, it would just confuse their own players. Plus, we are a pretty good team."

"Is Jenna going to Nebraska State, too?" Sam asked, changing the subject.

"I think so," Jack smiled. "She's the best. I think I'm in love with her."

"Remember when I said that you should date her?" Sam recalled.

"Yeah, so?" Jack countered.

"I hate to say I told you so, but," Sam sang.

Jack couldn't bear to hear him finish the end of that sentence so he lifted both legs and planted both feet on Sam's mattress springs. Jack kicked with such tremendous force, Sam's body was launched from the bed and flew straight up into the ceiling.

When the loud crash echoed through the house, both boys knew that their parents had to have heard it. They quickly pulled up their sheets and pretended to be asleep because they didn't want the 'get some sleep, you've got a big game' speech.

After a couple of minutes of hold-your-breath silence, Sam and Jack wished each other a very quiet 'good night'.

*

Jack looked down and checked his elbow pads. He'd had those pads since he was in the eighth grade. They were stained with a rainbow of colors and he could barely see any of their original color. He thought about how many times he had landed on those pads and how many scrapes and bruises they had prevented. He strapped them on, perhaps for the very last time. With his ankles taped and his should pads laced, Jack tucked his jersey into his pants.

With Jack still tying his shoes, the team and coaches broke for the door. Now all alone, Jack walked to the exit. As he was about to depart, he turned around and looked at the empty locker room one more time. He paused and a rush of adrenaline came over him. He vowed that his final game would be his best.

The Townies won the coin toss and received the opening kickoff. With the ball on the twenty-two, the Townies began their first possession.

When the Townies came to the line, Jack saw what was coming. Jack stepped up behind Ken and moved him out wider. With a sweep to the Screaming Eagles' left side, the defenders swarmed the ball and ran the ball carrier down for a loss of three yards. The next play was a counter draw. The Screaming Eagles didn't bite and Jack and Ken wrestled the tailback down for no gain. One third and thirteen, the Townies threw a quick out that fell incomplete.

The Screaming Eagles had won the first battle and their fans cheered happily when the defense left the field.

Coach Dawson knew that Sacred Heart wouldn't have an easy time on offense. The Townies were much bigger than the Screaming Eagles and welcomed the opportunity to attack a freshman quarterback. Coach Dawson believed that he could win the game with his defense and vowed not to lose it on offense. He called three consecutive running plays off tackle and on fourth and one the Screaming Eagles had to punt.

After the teams' offenses struggled to move through the first quarter, the game was tied 0-0 heading into the second. The Townies drew first blood when they returned the

Screaming Eagles' fourth punt sixty-four yards for a touchdown. Down by seven, Coach Dawson had no choice but to change his strategy and open up his offense.

On the next series, Sam threw on first down. When Tanner made a diving catch for twelve yards, the Sacred Heart players began to feel more confident. On the next play, Singleton broke a pitch out for nineteen more yards. Then, from the Townie forty, Sam threw a bomb to Shaffer for a touchdown.

The teams went into the half tied at seven, but the Screaming Eagles had renewed hope and left the field with momentum.

When the teams came out for the second half, Jack inspired the offensive line to block like bulldozers. He invited the left guard, John White, to double team the defensive end with him when Singleton ran off tackle. When Sam saw his brother and White block the end into the ground, he became giddy. On first down, Singleton gained eight.

On second down, Coach Dawson called the same play. Jack and John doubled the end again. When the play was over, Jack and John lay on top of the beaten defender six yards up the field. Coach Dawson was relentless. He called the play seven times in a row until Singleton burrowed into the end zone. The Screaming Eagles took a 14-7 lead.

What was a hard fought game turned into a rout on the next series. On third and six from their own twenty-nine, the Townies attempted to throw into double coverage. Mark picked off the pass and returned the ball for another touchdown.

At 21-7, late in the third quarter, the Townies became desperate and began to throw on every down. Jack, Tim and Ken teed off on the quarterback. When they didn't stunt, Jack would come on a straight blitz. Jack sacked the Townie quarterback twice on the next series, making it fourth and twenty-five.

After the punt, Sam took the team to pay dirt with a mix of run and pass plays covering forty-eight yards in six plays. Now at 28-7, well into the fourth quarter, the Screaming Eagles knew the game was decided and relaxed. Their perfect season and state title were in the bank.

To the delight of the Screaming Eagles' faithful, Coach Dawson removed the seniors from the game with 1:51 left. Jack and his friends sat on the bench and watched the time expire in both the game and their careers. Jack had never seen a game from this prospective and it gave him time to absorb the finality of it all.

It was over. The season, the smells and the sounds were all but gone. This was the final game and Jack felt a great sense of relief. He had done it. He had lived up to all of the expectations. This championship was the pinnacle of all of his accomplishments and now he felt a tremendous weight was lifted from his shoulders. He could relax and enjoy himself without any remorse or guilt. Jack was at peace with himself.

When the time expired, the Screaming Eagles had won 28-13.

Jack and his teammates acknowledged the fans after the game at an award ceremony. Jack sought out his parents, coaches and teachers and thanked them each for supporting him and the team.

Jenna waited patiently for Jack to make his rounds, waving to him to let him know where she was. Jack was generous with his time but he finally made it over to Jenna and gave her a big hug.

"Good game, Jack," Jenna complimented.

"Thanks," Jack responded. "It's only good if you have someone to share it with."

Jenna smiled and pulled Jack in for a big kiss.

Jenna opened her eyes and saw Mark, Ken, and Tim standing together at the middle of the field. Jack saw them, too.

"You should go be with your friends," Jenna suggested.

Jack smiled at Jenna, hugged her, and ran out to the center of the field.

When Jack joined the trio, they intertwined their arms and butted their heads against each other. They yelled and screamed with uninhibited joy.

"I'm going to miss it," Ken confessed.

"Me, too. But I'll miss you guys more than the game," Jack confided.

"I love you guys," Tim cried, making fun of Jack and Ken.

"It doesn't get any better than this," Mark proclaimed, "to win the state title with your best friends. We will remember this forever. Here's to us."

The boys took turns giving each other one final high five to commemorate the occasion.

When the four boys turned to walk off the field, Tim asked, "Where's Sam?"

The boys looked around and saw him sitting on the bench kissing Sarah.

"Would you look at that?" Tim said, pointing at the couple.

Shaking his head, Jack said, "That is so embarrassing."

"Doesn't our school have some kind of rule against that?" Mark asked the group.

"I don't know, but it just doesn't seem right," Ken added.

"Let's get him!" Tim yelled as the boys broke into a sprint for the bench.

Hearing the cry, Sam bolted from his perch and ran for his life.

Eventually, the foursome ran down the puny freshman and tackled him. Then, one at a time, they took turns working him over until Ken grabbed his underpants and gave him a ball busting wedgie. It was funny until Sam's underwear ripped under the stress. Then, it became hysterical to the four seniors when Ken was able to remove Sam's underpants entirely. Sam was only able to escape when the four fell to the grass in a fit of laughter.

*

Eight months later, Jack and Jenna packed what they could into Jack's Firebird. It was a steamy August day and the couple was waiting for a passing thunderstorm to clear the area before they began their trek across the country to Nebraska.

Jack's parents had given him a farewell party the evening before and all of his friends had come by to wish him good luck. Now, all that remained were his parents and his brother to say goodbye.

The storm was over and the couple headed for the door. Jack's family followed the couple down the driveway. Once Jack put Jenna in the car, he turned to his family.

"I love you, son," Mrs. Bowden said, putting her arms around her eldest son.

"I love you, too, Mom. I'll be back soon."

When they ended their embrace, Jack's father offered his hand. "Have a safe trip."

Jack stepped in and hugged his father.

After his father stepped back, Jack reached out for Sam's hand. "I'll miss you."

"I'll miss you, too, Jack," Sam answered, shaking Jack's hand.

Jack put the car in reverse and backed down the driveway. His family didn't move. They stood where he left them and waved as the car accelerated down the street.

"That was fun," Jack said, wiping a tear away from his eye.

Once they were out of sight, Jenna got excited.

"Let me drive?" she begged.

Jack had recently taught Jenna how to drive his car and couldn't think of any reason not to, so he pulled over and they switched places. Now Jack was able to relax as the car sped up Route 1 to the I-95 interchange.

As Jenna threw the car into fourth gear, she screamed with joy. Jack thought her happiness reflected her newfound independence. She was on her own and wanted to celebrate life to the fullest. She turned up the radio to its maximum volume and sang with the music. Her body danced back and forth helping Jack to overcome his sadness.

When Jenna crested a hill exceeding the speed limit by twenty miles per hour, Jack cautioned her. "You'd better ease up on the gas, Little Miss Lead Foot!"

Jenna just laughed.

Then up ahead on the sidewalk, Jack saw Wendy Thompson walking toward them. It was her. He was sure of it. He couldn't mistake her beautiful body and her perfect hair. She was walking with Sue Rich. He didn't want to say anything because he didn't want to dredge up bad memories of times passed that would dominate their conversation for the next ten hours. He looked the other way and made an irrelevant comment about the apartment complex on their left.

Jenna didn't blink. She, too, recognized Wendy and drove the car straight for her. Not hearing Jack's comment, she veered left missing Wendy and Sue by a mere five feet. Jenna, however, didn't miss the six inch deep puddle that stood adjacent to the two girls. Jenna sent a wave of the muddy water over Wendy and Sue. Jack turned his head to watch the two girls scream as they were soaked from head to toe. Wendy swore at them at the top of her lungs as the car sped away.

Laughing at Jenna's stunt, Jack finally said in realization, "Holy crap! She's going to think that was me."

Jenna turned toward Jack, smiled, and said, "*I know.*"

ABOUT THE AUTHOR

Mark Dengel was born in Ottawa, Kansas and graduated from Kansas State University prior to joining the Navy in 1986. After four years of active duty, he married and settled down in Warwick, Rhode Island. He went back to school and received his Master's Degree from Rhode Island College. He has taught middle school science for the past 18 years and is currently a teacher at Park View Middle School in Cranston RI. He has been married for 22 years and has three children. Mark retired from the US Naval Reserve in 2006.